MILFORD ELEMENTARY

BOOK ONE IN THE GWENDOLYN STRONG SMALL TOWN COZY MYSTERY SERIES

J A HODA

Copyright © 2022 by J A Hoda

All rights reserved.

No part of this book may be reproduced in any form or by any electronic or mechanical means, including information storage and retrieval systems, without written permission from the author, except for the use of brief quotations in a book review. All names are fictitious. Any resemblance to real persons is purely coincidental.

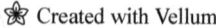 Created with Vellum

MILFORD ELEMENTARY:

Book One in the Gwendolyn Strong Small Town Cozy
Mystery Series
By J.A. Hoda

CHAPTER ONE

I am crying on what is normally the happiest day of the year for me.

I'm not talking about Christmas, with the mayhem of four generations unwrapping presents simultaneously, or repeatedly sneaking tiny slices of my stepmother's rum-laden fruit cake.

And I'm not talking about my birthday. Some would argue that my birthday should be my happiest day, but only three other people know the truth. After my sixth birthday, I was content to play the game and blow out the candles and make a wish that never came true.

No, today I am bawling because it's the first day of school and I'm not teaching for the first time in over thirty-five years. My body wracks in convulsions as the dam holding back my emotions breaks apart, and I am swept away in the flood.

My husband, Ken, put on the coffee this humid, late summer morning. He filled his thermos and then drove a couple of towns over to the big box home improvement store to get materials he needs for his latest customer. He is Milford's most trusted remodeler and does renovations like nobody's business. The city folks line up months in advance and pay big-city money for his craftsmanship on their fixer-uppers. He offered to stick around this morning, knowing how difficult today would be for me. We've been married for thirty-three years, so he knows my moods by now. I declined, but how I wish he found an excuse to tarry. Would I have kept up a brave face had he stayed, or would I have melted into his sinewy yet gentle arms, sobbing into his flannel work shirt?

Everything was as it should be this summer, like it had been for the last three and a half decades, until last Monday night—or was it early Tuesday morning? It's been a blur.

The school board was under siege by angry parents with the union attorneys giving the town folks all the ammunition. In the end, after a bitterly contested vote, the board decided to close Milford Elementary and eliminate seven teaching positions, custodians, and the school nursing office. It was not lost on the agitated crowd that the principal, who was not in the union, was spared and would become more overhead at the regional school district's administration building outside of town.

I was the senior of two kindergarten teachers in the district. I came to Milford as a student intern my last year at college and taught this magical grade, never having the desire to teach any other grade or subject. Where else do you get nap time after lunch? I would smile at those academics who thought I should strive to teach more erudite classes like chemistry at the academic high school or culinary at the vocational-technical school. I taught kindergarten for thirty-five years and treated it like a calling. Sometimes it could be monotonous, like on beautiful summery days in June added to make up for snow days, but mostly, I couldn't believe they paid me a living wage with benefits and the entire summer off for doing what I loved to do. I was excited about going to school every day.

Everyone expected I would exert my hard-earned seniority to keep my job, but I spoke in a clear, unwavering voice. I said

MILFORD ELEMENTARY

Christine Flaherty was a fine kindergarten teacher, and at twenty-four, she had the energy and qualifications to carry on the legacy started by Emelina Bidwell seventy-five years earlier. I had brought Christine along the way Emelina taught me, and it was time for fresh blood to take over. I said that out loud, and in the crowd, I spotted my now newly minted centenarian mentor Emelina beaming.

So, I stunned everybody, including myself, by offering to take the golden parachute package and be laid off in place of my protégé.

Christine's job was safe. I promised to fill in when she needed me, given that she was pregnant with her second. Afterwards, Christine and her husband, Ron, a former student, each hugged me unabashedly, while over their shoulders, I received the stink eye from our union rep. Union rules stipulated last hired, first fired. I was bucking the union. I shrugged. Whaddya gonna do in a small town?

The closing of the school was a shock, although it shouldn't have been. Declining enrollments while trying to maintain an aging facility were not new to the folks here. Church congregations and their elders had faced the same problems, and several beautiful houses of worship sat shuttered.

The school board failed to consider the nostalgia of a small-town school where generations of taxpayers had attended. I paid little attention to the too little, too late calls to demand a referendum. I had a garden to weed, tomatoes to can, and an upstairs bedroom to repaint. So, I kept myself busy as the week flew by.

Parents know what it's like to put their kid on the school bus for their first school day. For some of the children, already veterans of one or two day-care facilities, the separation is no big deal, but for others it is traumatic for both the child and the parents. They had been inseparable since the child's birth. The kids can pick up on the parents' separation anxiety too and feed off it.

On the first day of school, I would welcome the kids and the parents to kindergarten. Many of the recent years' parents had been my students, and without exception, they told their children that when they were in my class; they loved it.

For many children, the first day of school can be awful. It was my job to make it awesome. Whether I sat on a chair in a circle or on the floor that first day, I made sure they did not feel abandoned, and they knew this was a safe place for them to make friends. No one should be terrified by their first day in school. The importance of making the children feel welcome on their first day was never lost on me. I wasn't there this morning for them, and I could feel the ache in my gut like I had eaten bad shellfish.

I am Mrs. Strong to most of the people in town, Gwen to my friends and colleagues, and Gwendolyn to my husband on those rare occasions when he is cross with me. Today, I am a ship in a tempest, without a rudder, breaking apart on the rocky coast.

What am I going to do?

I am Mom to my son, Wesley and my daughter, Erin. He's single and is an accountant for the electric company. She is a stay-at-home mom with three precious children and a good marriage to Darren, a financial wealth manager. They live about forty-minutes away. She home-schools the older two and has an interesting part-time job she can do anywhere with an internet connection.

She's calling me now. It's uncanny how she always knows when to check in on me.

I go first. "Hi, honey. How are the kids?"

"We're stuck inside this morning but managing. How are you?"

"I didn't expect today to hit me so hard." How much do I tell her? "I wasn't planning on retiring for another nine years. It all happened so suddenly." I take the middle road. "Truth be told, I am not processing it all very well."

"I can't begin to imagine how you feel. Thirty-five years is a long time of doing something, and now you're not."

"It was my choice, Erin, and I did the right thing. Time to pass on the torch and move on."

"Any ideas, Mom?"

"Not a clue. I have time before I need to work again. The school gave me a lump sum payout, and that doesn't even include all my unused sick time."

"You were never sick."

"I accumulated the most days of any current employee. Only Emelina had more."

"Cha-ching! That should tide you over for a while."

"I know that I could plop down on the couch eating Cheetos and bingeing Netflix, but that would get awfully boring. I can't sit around all day and wait for your dad to get home, and I don't want to just do something for the sake of keeping busy. I still can contribute."

"Like volunteer stuff?" my daughter asks.

"I don't know. Nothing is really grabbing me."

"What's your favorite movie, Mom?"

"You know it's *Groundhog Day*. Why?"

"Bill Murray's character didn't figure it out right away either. You already have an open heart. It will come to you faster than you think."

I raised a smart daughter. "My pupils are in good hands with Christine Flaherty. I will call her after dinner and ask how her first day went. Right now, I have to go for a walk and clear my head." A brisk stroll around town always makes me feel better.

Erin tells me, "Do yourself a favor and don't let your feet walk you by the school. It won't do you any good."

"Yes, Mrs. LeGrande," I reply. I raised a good mother, too.

"Maybe I'll buy something special at the grocery store and have it on the table when your father comes home."

"Dad will like that, but I'm sure he will take you out to eat if you change your mind."

"Love 'em and hug 'em, honey." I always end my calls with Erin that way.

"Will do, Mom."

I decided to walk about Milford. It has a busy few blocks of downtown where the state highways intersect before taking the truck traffic and tourists to the interstate on the outskirts of town. I avoid those streets and navigate along alleys and residential roads.

I feel like I am playing hooky. School is in session, and I am not there. Last year, Erin and I spent a long weekend and Thanksgiving in New Haven, but I can't recall any other time when my fanny wasn't firmly planted in Room #1 of the 106-year-old school building. Instead of feeling better, I feel like a goldfish flopping on the ground outside of the fishbowl. I breathed easier on the climbing parts of the Appalachian Trail than today on the warm sidewalks of my hometown. The growing tightness in my chest and the stars in my eyes warn me this walk is not a good idea, but I keep going anyways.

CHAPTER TWO

"Gwen, honey, are you okay?"

The face of Emelina Bidwell forms in front of me. I am inside an air-conditioned room. It is quiet and cool. Natural light streams from the windows. Behind her is the concerned face of a man I vaguely recall. He has long gray hair tied in a ponytail and a beard of the same color. Emelina, at 100 years old, is still spry and very mobile. Evidently, she is also very flexible. She is wearing yoga clothes, and I am laying prone on a yoga mat in a yoga studio.

Ken had redone this house so that the non-bearing wall separating the living room and dining room was removed. He installed hardwood flooring and restored the supporting walls to their original plaster lathe. I brought a few hand tools here to Ken last summer while he worked on this rehab.

I now remember the ponytailed man as the owner, Abe Schatz. He contracted Ken to turn the downstairs front rooms into the studio and update the kitchen in the back. Ken told me that Abe was a commodities trader from the city who had burned out on the hustle. Divorced and estranged from his adult children, he changed his life and now offers five-dollar drop-in classes for meditation and yoga in the mornings and evenings.

As I sit up, I notice a dozen other people milling about. Their faces show concern as well.

"I'm okay," I say too soon, then close my eyes to the swirling stars.

"You gave us quite the scare," Emelina says. "We were in tree pose when you knocked on the door. You looked as white as a ghost, dear."

"I'm not handling the first day of school very well, I suppose." I open my eyes again, and the room stops spinning this time.

"Here's a cup of chamomile tea with lemon," Abe tells me. "Drink."

I notice that my sneakers had been removed when I sit cross-legged. I take the tea and sip slowly, blowing on it.

The yogis nod at me as they make their way to the door. Class is over, and I am the reason.

"It's normal to feel this way, dear," Emelina says. "I knew for a few years before I decided to retire what I wanted to do. Then you came along, and I knew it was time. I was waiting for the right student-teacher to take my place." She places a hand on my knee. "You surprised everybody at the school board meeting the other night, including yourself, I take it."

"I didn't have a Plan B, and it all hit me today. I didn't realize how emotional today was going to be."

"How's the tea?" Abe asks.

"Very calming," I reply.

"Would you like a raspberry scone? They're gluten-free."

Out of politeness, I am about to decline when Emelina says, "Yes, and I will have one too."

We sit cross-legged on mats drinking tea and eating scones. Emelina fills Abe in on my sudden decision to resign.

He says, "It was different for me. I had to stop doing what I was doing, or it would have killed me—or I would have killed myself. You chose to leave prematurely what you loved doing. That's a big difference."

"This is what you chose to do?" I ask.

"It chose me," he replies. "I needed to slow down my mind and listen to my body. I go back to the city every six months for a check-in with my doctor, and he's amazed at my numbers. I'm off all medications and am only taking a baby aspirin and a multivitamin. A better diet and the tea help."

"I'm in great shape. That's why I don't understand what happened to me," I tell them.

Abe smiles. "I'm no doctor, and I don't play one on TV, but I think you had an anxiety attack. I saw them all the time with clients when the stock market went into the toilet."

I chew and sip as I take in this sage advice.

"Does not being with the kids today bother you, or is it a fear of your future?" Emelina asks.

"Definitely not being with the kids for their first day of school. I've had no thoughts about what I want to do when I grow up. What did you do?"

"Everything. I said yes to everything. If I started thinking of myself as old and retired, do you think I would be in Abe's class today to catch you when you fell?"

"She makes me feel old," Abe says, winking at his oldest student.

"In the word *retired* is the word *tired*," Emelina says. "There are some days when I feel tired, and that's okay. Most days, I jump out of bed with a fresh twenty-four hours to play with." What did Erin say about *Groundhog Day?*

Abe adds, "I meditate, do yoga, skip breakfast, catch up on correspondence, have a light lunch, take a nap, work on a project, and make a nice dinner before the evening meditation and yoga class to finish the day. This routine grounds me and keeps me focused on what's important."

"What's that?"

"It's not horns honking, ambulance and police sirens all day, or cutthroat commodity trading, that's for sure." He smiles. "What's important is different for everybody. You will find out in due time."

Emelina tells me, "You said it yourself. The kids are in good hands with Christine. There is an entire world waiting for you out there to explore. What are you waiting for?"

I fell literally into the hands of my mentor in this spiritual space. I don't think Abe thinks of himself as a guru, but he is.

I stand on sturdy legs now and carry the teacup to a table next to a trash can, where I brush the crumbs from my shirt. "You both are what the doctor ordered. It is always good to see you, Emelina. Next time I drop in, Abe, it won't be so dramatic." I hug her and give Abe a fist-bump.

"Take care, honey," she says.

"Say hello to Ken for me," Abe adds.

The country market has what I am looking for. Bill the butcher is cutting the steaks special for me. Local farmer's corn, string beans, peaches are already in my basket. I will buy the vanilla ice cream last. Ken loves to grill, and I'll do the veggies. Sliced peaches in melting ice cream in the screened-in porch is dessert. I will pull some mint from the garden for tea tonight.

I can't believe how the chamomile in that tea calmed me down. I was so fortunate to find Emelina and Abe when I did. I will explore with Ken about what the next third of my life might look like. My dad is doing okay at 81, but he and his recliner have become one lately, and he needs to move more. I hope to follow in my mentor's footsteps and hit triple digits, not spend the next part of my life tethered to a recliner.

"Hello, Mrs. Strong," I hear from down the paper goods aisle. It's Yvette Strohmeyer. She is due any day now and swore to me once that she would never carry another pregnancy through the summer. She was a student of mine from twenty years ago. She married Mike Strohmeyer, a sheriff and a student of mine from back then. Having chance meetings with my students or their parents at the store or around town is not uncommon. I always take the time to chat.

"Hi Yvette. How are you?" I say as she walks over. Yvette knows that I am looking for a real answer, not a polite response.

"Big as a house, miserable with this heat and humidity, and can't wait to become a mother."

"When's your due date?"

"Last Tuesday, Doctor Lockhart says not to worry. Everything is fine, she tells me."

"Pepperoni pizza worked for me. Erin was late, and I had a pepperoni pizza. At first, I thought it was heartburn at four in the morning, then my water broke, and off to the hospital we went. You don't want to hear how long I was in labor with her. They pulled her out kicking and then screaming."

"Why is it that every mother doesn't want to tell me about labor, other than that it's worth it?"

"Why do you think?"

"You always did that to us, Mrs. Strong. You always made us come up with the answer."

"So, Yvette, what's the answer to your question?" I smile as Bill finishes prepping the second rib eye.

"Here you go, Mrs. Strong," he says. "You and Ken will like these."

"Thanks, Bill."

I turn back to Yvette, who gives me her answer. "Because for every woman, it is different, and there is a reason it's called labor. The moms don't want me to be any more nervous than I am," she offers.

"That's part of it, but it is also indescribable to someone who has never experienced it. You will find the words to describe it when it's over as you stare at your precious baby."

"Thanks, Mrs. Strong. Hey, how come you aren't at school? Today's the first day, right?"

"I'm sorry to tell you, Yvette, that they closed Milford Elementary. They decided to shut it down for budgetary reasons."

"I didn't hear that. That's terrible. How many kids passed through there? I have so many memories, especially in your class."

"They combined the kindergartens, and I chose to resign rather than have them lay off the other teacher, who is also pregnant and had less seniority."

"Wow, she must have been happy to keep her job. Good jobs are hard to find in Milford. What are you going to do, Mrs. Strong?"

"They gave me a package, so I don't have to rush. It's been too much of a blur since it happened. I am nervous but excited, sort of like you, Yvette. I don't know what to expect."

"Whatever you decide, Mrs. Strong, you will be good at it, I know," Yvette tells me.

"Thanks," I say, happy for the affirmation of a former student.

Changing subjects, Yvette asks me, "Isn't that terrible about Jake Dawson?"

"I didn't hear. What happened?" Jake was a student of mine from the same class as Yvette. I try not to be alarmed when I hear bad news, so I work to keep a calm face.

"He died Friday night, the night before he was to get married."

"That's terrible!" I blurt out. "How?"

"They say he shot himself."

CHAPTER THREE

The wake that night for Jake Dawson takes up the largest parlor in the McSweeney funeral home. The parking lot is overflowing with classmates and friends waiting their turn to pay respects. His extended family takes up all the seats in the room. It will be a long night for them.

Ken understands from the note I left him why dinner was microwaveable leftovers. When he joins me in his best and only suit, we process in a long line, room to room. Flowers of every imaginable color and fragrance form an arch around the closed casket. Between us, we know almost everyone in attendance. The music is soft, the drapery luxurious. The period furniture is from the time after the Civil War when this mansion was built. The grand structure sits a few blocks from the town center. The property does not show the tired expression of a town that has seen its better days. Death is a steady business. The large oak tree in the center of the front lawn may be the oldest in all of Milford, and purple azaleas and crimson hydrangeas flank either side of the columned portico.

I kneel before the closed casket, and Ken does the same. I see a recent picture of Jake with a dress shirt and tie. He is smiling

MILFORD ELEMENTARY

the smile I remember from the first day of school when I told him that everything would be all right. He was the youngest of the Dawson family, and I told him his brothers and sisters had sat in the same chair he was sitting in that day. Of course, I wasn't sure if it was the exact wooden chair, but telling the youngest child that older siblings survived kindergarten always worked.

Kneeling there brings back memories of Jake as if it was yesterday. He was calmer and quieter than most of his class. The girls that year were more rambunctious than the boys. Maybe it had to do with sibling order or some other nurture versus nature argument, but the girls were a handful, as I recall. Jake was always willing to help me with handing out glue sticks, crayons, and blunt scissors. He was taught manners at home, and the other kids learned about "please" and "thank you" from him and a few others.

Ken nudges my elbow to bring me back to the present. We stand and make our way to Mabel and Warren, parents burying their youngest.

"I am so sorry, Mabel," I tell her.

"Oh, Mrs. Strong, it seems like just yesterday that I sent him off to kindergarten."

We hold each other close.

"I remember Jake's first day of school," I say. "He was so happy."

"He was always happy, Mrs. Strong. We had been with him at the rehearsal dinner, and he was so excited about getting married, and now he is dead. I don't understand."

"We both watched him grow up. I was speechless when I found out," I tell her.

"We'll know more after we get the results of the autopsy," Warren says over her shoulder.

Ken reaches for his hand. "My condolences, Warren. If there is anything I can do, just give me a holler."

"Had to be drugs," Warren says resolutely. "He never would have done it in his right mind."

We remain silent for a moment, contemplating that possibility. Drugs were the X factor that explained a Jekyll and Hyde change in so many people around town. Unlike with alcohol, the changes were often swift and dramatic.

"He drank only a little Friday night, as he was getting married the next day. He didn't want to be hungover on his wedding day," Mabel tells me. "None of this makes sense."

"I'll come by in a couple days," I promise her. "If you need anything." I nod to her, and she nods back as Ken and I move down the line.

We know Jake's brothers and sisters and are introduced to their partners. We repeat our condolences. I flash back to each brother and sister's time in my classroom. Each relationship is unique, as each one of them is different. They were vulnerable then and are shaken to the core now, and they look to me for strength and steadiness as their worlds fill with deep sadness and shock. Everyone repeats that Jake had everything to live for. I have a little training in grief counseling and promise each one that I am there for them. If they want to talk, I am available. No job to go to in the morning or for the foreseeable future makes my promises real.

Next, we talk to aunts, uncles, and cousins, the locals we know and the out-of-towners we are introduced to. The Dawson family tree fills out. Either Ken has done work for them, or I taught them in school. A small town has a way of magnifying relationships. A funeral, more than a wedding, cements that feeling of interconnectedness, as the dead don't have a guest list. Anybody can mourn.

"Go ahead, Ken, I'll catch up with you outside in a few," I say as I spot Jake's fiancée.

Sharon McGrath is sitting by herself on a sofa. She is utterly alone in her thoughts. She spots me and stands. She is as tall as I, five-foot-ten and much thinner than my 135 pounds. My soft Afro and darker skin contrasts with her tied-back blonde hair falling limply to mid-back and her mourning pallor. A simple black dress hangs on her frame.

"Mrs. Strong," she says, "thank you for coming."

There is more to that greeting, like she is the little girl who trusted me with her feelings all those years ago. "Sharon, I am so sorry for you."

"He wouldn't do this to himself, and he didn't do it to me."

Jilting a bride on her wedding day is terrible; a groom killing himself to avoid getting married is almost unheard of. "You're right, Sharon. It doesn't make sense."

She pulls me in close and whispers, "My parents didn't come. They have some weird thoughts about suicide and blame Jake for robbing them of a wedding." She fixes me with a trembling gaze that tells me everything. She isn't officially Mrs. Dawson, and Jake's death the night before they were to get married raises all kinds of questions. I could tell she feels like a leper on the day when she should have been a bride in wedded bliss on her honeymoon.

The school district had some arcane rules about hugging children when they were in pain, but nothing prohibits me from hugging her closely today. She sobs as I hold her. I don't care that the Dawson clan looks on or that townsfolk who came to pay their respects watch me comfort her. It is the right thing to do at exactly the right time. Sharon held it all inside until somebody she trusted came in, and that person is me, her kindergarten teacher.

We slowly make our way to the bathrooms and kick out a couple of bored teenagers on their cellphones.

"Thank you, Mrs. Strong, for saving me. I thought I was about to explode."

"I can't imagine what you are going through. I don't know the words to comfort you."

"You being here is enough. You were the only one to ask me how I was doing." She blows her nose and stares in the mirror. "Look at me, I'm a mess."

"It's okay."

Sharon blasts the cold water and scoops handfuls onto her face over the sink. Staring into the basin she says, "My dad told me that the photographer and DJ refused to give them back the deposits. Like I friggin' care." She places both hands on the marble sink as her face drips.

I hand her a paper towel. She blots her face, then lifts her head and composes herself with a couple of breaths. "We were best friends in grade school, and he took me to both my proms. We wanted to get started on our careers before we got married. He didn't get cold feet, Mrs. Strong."

My thoughts drift back to when they played together at recess. My students were on the playground when the other grades were outside, and I watched years of my students growing up before my eyes. Conversations with other teachers filled in why some kids were misbehaving. Jake and Sharon were never mentioned.

"Jake and his best man Brian were inseparable at the Vo-Tech. They wanted to bang on fenders for the rest of their lives. They had a good business," Sharon adds after blowing her nose again loudly. "They had a great future and talked about building another bay. Does that sound like somebody wishing he were dead?"

I hand her another paper towel. I knew that the boys own an auto body shop and were making a go of it. I say, "They fixed my father's car after his last oops before we convinced him to stop driving."

Her voice is stronger now. "We said good night after the rehearsal dinner. I wanted to get a good night's sleep. His groomsmen wanted to have one last drink with him back at the cabin. He kissed me and told me he loved me and wished we were already married. Does that sound like somebody who would blow his head off?"

"It doesn't," I tell her. "Mr. Dawson was wondering about drugs."

"No way, Mrs. Strong. I would have known if he was doing drugs. I could drink more than him, and whatever we did in high school was years behind us. Brian handled the paint booth, as Jake would get nauseous around it if they didn't ventilate well enough."

She reapplies her makeup. Dark mascara over reddened eyes doesn't make for a good look, but she is composed. "I sat there for two hours until you came in, Mrs. Strong. I made my presence known to the family. Now I will grieve by myself."

"You don't have to grieve by yourself. You're not alone, Sharon. I am here for you."

"I know, Mrs. Strong. You've always been there for us."

We hug again, then walk out of the bathroom. A line of thin-lipped women has formed in the hallway.

I find Ken outside in the parking lot talking with some other fellows and tug on his arm.

"Do you think Dairy Queen is still open?" I whisper to him. "It's been a heck of a day."

CHAPTER FOUR

Many years ago, before Ken and I were married, we would get frisky at our favorite parking spot down by the river, but tonight we're here sharing a peanut butter sundae with two spoons. Different kind of frisky. Late summer thunderstorms power the swift current. When our children were teenagers, we would tell them we were going out to watch the submarine races. "Ew," Erin would say. "Mom," Wesley would add, making a face like the one time I made him eat lima beans. We just needed an excuse to get out of the house, and they were old enough to fend for themselves. We'd come down here to stare at the river and be together.

The half-moon reflects off the undulating water. Our windows are up. We learned the hard way all those years ago when mosquitos (which I swear were the size of hummingbirds) were attracted to my bare skin like it was nectar. The truck's AC cools us as we share the sundae with the quiet calm of a long and mostly happy marriage.

"How was your day, Hon?" I ask.

"Hot. The fans I brought to the farmhouse didn't move the air at all." He is doing a kitchen and bathroom update for a city doctor looking to retire to the country.

"Did you stay hydrated?"

"Coffee."

"That doesn't count," I remind him.

"Sure, it does. I made it with water, didn't I?"

We have this argument all the time. "Well, I didn't drink enough water this morning before I went for a walk. I got dizzy, and luckily found Emelina at Abe Schatz's yoga studio. He says hello, by the way." That part is true. I fail to mention my crying jag or the tightness in my chest. I don't want to worry my man.

He finishes his scoop and asks, "Were you okay?"

"Tea and a raspberry gluten-free scone fixed me right up." Moving on to avoid further inquiry I say, "I had grand intentions of having you grill a couple steaks, while I did the corn and string beans—Bill the butcher says hello too—when I met Yvette Strohmeyer at the store. That's how I learned about Jake."

"Talk about a rollercoaster for Mabel and Warren," he says. "To go from planning a wedding for your youngest to standing next to his casket. I can't imagine how his family is dealing with it."

"Sharon McGrath, his bride-to-be, was utterly alone in her despair. I did my best to comfort her. She doesn't want to believe that Jake killed himself."

He ropes me back to the earlier part of the day. "I never got to ask you how you felt about not being in the classroom."

"It hit me harder than I thought it would. I really missed being there for the kids on their first day of school. I felt like I was playing hooky when I went for my walk. Emelina and Abe talked me through it, though."

"Any thoughts on what to do?"

"Besides car-racing, hang-gliding, and learning to play the violin?" I wink at him. "Nothing else pops up right now. Emelina says retirement is a state of mind, and Abe advised that my future purpose would come to me in time."

"No rush, no pressure from me. The kids are doing fine, and we have enough saved in the emergency fund."

"The kids *are* doing fine," I repeat. "We should call them and tell them about Jake." I want to do that as much for me as for them, to reassure myself that my kids are well, my grandkids are well, and we have much to be grateful for. Small towns are not immune to sudden deaths. A car wreck, a heart attack, and yes, even death by suicide are all parts of the cycle of life here.

I hold the ice cream boat in my hands and don't give in to the temptation to lick it clean while Ken drives back to our latest fixer upper. He speculates on houses in town. We live in them while he fixes them up so he can later flip them. He's done that since Wesley moved out. Buy low. Sell high. The locations of each were always within walking distance of Milford Elementary. I guess he can widen that circle now.

"What's wrong, Mom?"

"Nothing, Wes. Can't a mother call her son to see how he's doing?"

"I'm fine."

"Okay, how's work coming along?"

"Fine. I'm really busy with projects all the time."

"That's good. Do you like them?"

"Did you call me up to talk about my job?"

"No, honey, not really. There was a sudden death in town this week. Did you know Jake Dawson?"

"Kinda. I went to school with his sister, Candace. I think we were a couple of years apart. He went to Vo-Tech, didn't he?"

"Yes. He and Brian Yelito have an auto body shop in town and fixed your grandfather's car. We went to his viewing tonight. Jake was twenty-five."

There is silence now. Wesley has more patience than me. He's not even asking me how Jake died. "I just wanted to hear your voice," I say. "Do you think you will make it home for Sunday dinner?"

"Not sure. I'm really busy lately. Can I take a raincheck?"

"Let me know if you can make it, so I can set a place for you."

"Will do, Mom. Gotta go."

I say, "Love you." Not sure if he hangs up first.

I call Erin. She answers on the second ring. "Hi Mommy, what's up?"

"Just checking in on my favorite daughter."

"I'm your only daughter," Erin teases me back.

"How are the kids?"

"We got them down about a half hour ago. Just finished cleaning the kitchen and family room. Getting everything ready for the morning. I'm a little late logging on to work."

"How well do you remember the Dawson family?" I ask.

"I was in the same class as Warren Jr. Didn't they have like six kids?"

"Five, their youngest was Jake."

"Was?"

"Your father and I went to his viewing tonight. They say that he shot himself."

"Accidentally?"

"No, they are calling it a death by suicide."

"That's terrible."

"He was to get married to Sharon McGrath. Did you know her?"

"Vaguely."

"Both Jake and Sharon were in the same grade. They were

always together. He died Friday night, and they were to get married the next day. "

"Oh my God! That's so sad," she says.

"Both his mother and Sharon don't know what to believe. Warren, Jake's father, is saying that it had to be drugs, but Sharon is adamant that Jake was not taking any drugs. He appeared happy at the rehearsal dinner and wasn't drinking much."

She says, "The autopsy should include a toxicology report, but they don't always check for all the drugs, just the usual suspects like marijuana, cocaine, heroin."

Before her part-time internet job, Erin was a true crime junkie. She knows the story of every serial killer since Jack the Ripper. The girl has an encyclopedic memory. She had inhaled the Oxygen, Investigation Discovery, and Court TV channels. Then she began listening to true crime podcasts and joining their closed Facebook groups. We had even attended a cold case symposium on a mother-daughter weekend last year. She is the right person to talk to.

"I can't make sense of it, honey," I tell her.

"What do you think happened, Mom?"

"I'm having trouble believing that Jake committed death by suicide."

"Why?"

"I've known him and have seen him around town since he was five years old."

"People change."

"I know."

"What else?"

I taught my daughter well. "His mother can't offer any reasons."

"And?"

"His fiancée said he didn't shoot himself."

"Who were the last people to see him?"

"His groomsmen wanted to have a drink with him back at his cabin."

"When did they last see him alive?"

"Sharon said he died around midnight."

"How does she know the time?"

"I don't know," I say.

"What else did Sharon tell you?"

"He blew his head off."

"And the last time she saw him?"

I recall the bloodshot eyes and mascara-covered face in the funeral home's bathroom mirror. "Erin, it was the rehearsal dinner." Can I separate my feeling at the viewing from what was said to me there? For Jake's sake, I suck it up.

"Let's assume that I am right," I say. The true crime junkie and her mother have had some practice at this. We reverse roles and she plays Watson to my Holmes. "For the sake of argument, let's say that Jake Dawson didn't shoot himself."

"Who did then?" Erin asks.

"Are you asking the right question?" I prod.

"No, you're right. Why was he killed?"

"What else?" I ask.

"Why the night before his marriage?"

"What reason did somebody have to kill Jake the night before he was to marry?" I pose a statement as question to her.

"Because something changes when he gets married," she says.

"That *something* gets him killed," I respond.

We sit with this working hypothesis. Erin is offering no other questions or solutions.

"What are you going to do now?" she asks me.

"Sleep on it or try to, at least," I reply.

"How's it feel to be back in the sleuthing saddle again, Mom?"

"That was just beginner's luck."

"Beginner's luck, my derriere. You remember what the FBI agent said? You have a gift. Which reminds me—I have to get to work."

Thanks to Erin's digging on a cold case last year, the number two person in the FBI offered her a part-time civilian gig working with a hand-picked intelligence analyst on cases having huge social media footprints. Erin has the smarts and drive to succeed at her task. She's a woman possessed when she digs into a case. Since then, I just viewed my contribution as a fluke. I was Erin's mom. But a gift? I don't know about that.

It's late, I realize. "Okay, honey. Love 'em and hug 'em for me."

"Hugs and kisses for your grandbabies in the morning, I promise," she says.

I head off to bed and slip in next to Ken. I stare at the ceiling with racing thoughts as I toss and turn. What if I'm right? What if Jake was murdered? I can't get comfortable no matter how I position myself. This is not like me. I am electric. Ken has to get up in the morning. I'm exhausted, but I can't stop thinking about Jake's death.

I slide out of bed and go down to the kitchen and brew some chamomile tea with lemon, then go to my scrapbook. I slowly flip through thirty-five years of kindergarten class photos with the children's names written under each photo. Each class brings back a flood of memories.

Finally, I arrive at the one I am looking for. I take the page with Jake, Sharon, Yvette, and Mike's smiling faces in the group photo and carefully remove it from the binder. I tiptoe upstairs past our bedroom on the creaky wooden floors and down the hallway to a spare room I use for my workspace. I center the photo on the corkboard where I used to keep lesson plans, and with a piece of chalk, I write on the slate board next to it: *Jake Dawson. Suicide?*

MILFORD ELEMENTARY

I contemplate what Erin said about having a gift. Can I be there for just one child on this first day of school? He needs me to get to the truth. If it's a death by suicide, why did he do it? If it's not death by suicide? That answer may come from one of those kids smiling back at me in the photo.

CHAPTER FIVE

What was I thinking? And why am I thinking?
I am supposed to be meditating in Abe's seven a.m. meditation period. Ten of us sit on cushions or in chairs in a semicircle facing him. This morning is cooler, with the sweet, dry cross breeze giving me goosebumps. I keep returning to my conversations the previous evening and not my breath. Slowly, though, my racing thoughts subside.

I am left with a feeling of not being good enough for the task, and I am not talking about meditation. If I was preparing for class today, I'd be thinking about the kids and what we would do, as I have done it for thirty-five years. That routine allowed me to focus on the kids.

I take a deep breath, pause, and count backwards from eleven, then I breathe in for a seven-count followed by a pause and let it out for a measured eleven count. Breathe and count. This is simple enough, except because these darn thoughts keep bubbling up. I don't have a lesson plan for what I am contemplating. How can I allow myself to believe that I can investigate Jake's death? I have no lesson plan; I have no guidebooks.

I drift into a conversation with Erin in my head. *No, Erin, last year we were presented with the facts of a twenty-year-old murder in New Haven. We visited the crime scenes and saw how the police decided to put the puzzle together with pieces that didn't fit, and all I did was point out the obvious. Everything was laid out for us.*

In for seven, at the pause. I feel the need to finish that thought. *No, honey, it's not a gift, it was just common sense. The cops decided on a couple of suspects before they even started their investigation.*

Out for eleven. I take a deep, cleansing breath. *Yes, honey, an FBI agent was interested in the case and asked us personally to get involved.*

In for seven, pause. *But that doesn't mean I know what to do.*

Out for eleven. I screw up the count and have to suck in air with a gulp. Why did I pick this day to meditate? Why did I pick this day to poke around a supposed death by suicide? I could think about my garden, but I am mulling over what I know so far.

I open my eyes and see Abe's tranquil half smile. The others are calmly breathing rhythmically. This isn't rocket science, but there is something about sitting here quietly and focusing on my breath. It's different from gardening, where I place all my attention on the task at hand, whether it's turning the soil, planting, or weeding. Rather than let the thoughts drift away like puffy white clouds in a clear blue sky, I turn them over against the backdrop of a singular premise.

Jake was shot to death.

I am startled when Abe sounds the bell. How long was I deep in thought about Jake? What started out as the slowest hour of my life went by quickly.

"This is a good time to stretch your legs if you are seated on a cushion," Abe says.

I uncross my legs and find out the hard way they've fallen asleep. Standing up is not an option right now, so I shake them out in front of me on the floor. I am surprised as Emelina pops right up and starts readying the room for yoga. I am going to try it, I decide. Years ago, the rec center sponsored an introductory course, but the instructor was a posture Nazi and I ended up quitting after the first session. She was from the city and didn't last long in Milford. Abe comes to his practice with reverence. It saved his life, and now he helps others improve their lives.

Eventually, the pins and needles from toes to buttocks subside, and I stand. I retrieve a mat, a blanket, and a thing called a bolster from the hardwood cubbies along the interior side wall, then mimic how the others set them up.

For the next hour, Abe talks us through seated, standing and relaxation poses. The guided meditation in corpse pose knocks me out, and for the second time in two days, Emelina and Abe hover above me as I wake up.

"That was wonderful," I say.

Again, Emelina pulls me to a seated position. "You look so relaxed."

"That was wonderful," I repeat, as much for them. Two and a half hours ago, I was a bundle of jangled nerves. Now I feel like jello. The tightness in my chest is gone. A warm softness radiates outward from my abdomen. Anything is possible.

"Not a bad way to start your day," Abe tells me.

"Not at all," I agree. I wipe down the mat, then roll it up and return it to the cubby along with the props. I linger until the last person leaves. Emelina notices my lingering and joins me.

Abe looks towards us, and we meet in the center of the room.

"I was wondering if you had a minute to talk with me," I start.

"I don't know, Gwen. I am a pretty busy lady," Emelina says.

"Sure, what's up?" Abe asks.

I take a deep breath and resolve to myself to speak plainly and directly. No beating around the bush. "Last year, my daughter Erin and I helped the FBI solve a murder in New Haven."

MILFORD ELEMENTARY

I watched both of their jaws drop while they raise their eyebrows in surprise.

"I figured that would grab your attention." I smile. "They were so impressed with Erin's skills they offered her a part-time, work-at-home job as a consultant. I won't bore you with the details. Repeatedly, the agent in charge of the investigation said that I also had a gift." I put air quotes around "gift." "She said that I had a way of looking at things as they really were. You teach kindergarten for thirty-five years the way we have," I nod to Emelina, who smiles knowingly, "and you see it written on the faces of the kids. There is no hiding what's happening in their heads. What you see is what you get. They haven't learned how to get cute with the truth yet."

"I think I know what you mean," he says. "There is some of that in sales. You get to read people if you do it long enough."

"Erin reminded me last night of my gift when I told her about how a student of mine from twenty years ago died recently. The official version is that he shot himself."

"But you don't think so," Emelina says.

"I didn't think so last night, but this morning I am not so sure."

"What changed?" Abe asks.

"Less about the facts and more about what I can do about it."

"Meaning what?" he asks.

"You mean you're getting cold feet," Emelina says before I can answer. My hundred-year-old former mentor is throwing down the gauntlet, and she's right. I don't have a great answer why now differs from last night.

"It was different in New Haven," I try to explain.

"You figured out something in a town you've never been to before and where you didn't know anybody. Am I missing something?"

Of course, she is right. Between us, we probably know all the locals and half the newbies. I've lived here since college. "It is still an active investigation; I would be intruding," I tell them.

Abe shakes his head. "That poop doesn't flush." His soft eyes drill into mine.

"So, it would be better to wait twenty years and then solve it?" Emelina says with an innocent grin. It is allowable for centenarians to zing you; they've earned that right.

"Ask yourself why you need to know what really happened," Abe adds.

"Because I owe it to my former student to find out if he really committed death by suicide and why."

"And?" Abe prods me.

"Because I think I can discover the answer."

"And if he didn't shoot himself?" Abe lets the question hang in the air like my intimates flapping on a clothesline.

CHAPTER SIX

The monotony of the glossy white-trimmed windows and eggshell white walls in the Milford Community Church color scheme are broken up by the colorful flags of our country and state mounted next to the pulpit, where the silver-haired Reverend Steele is delivering the eulogy. I stare at the closed economy silver coffin in the center aisle of this non-denominational house of worship. Many attending would have been here for the wedding wearing colorful outfits. Instead, they have donned their darkest suits or most somber dresses. The mood is hard to judge. A death by suicide leaves a lot of questions.

As Jeremiah Steele pauses, I hear more clearly the sobbing coming from Jake's family directly in front of him. They would have sat on the other side of the aisle for the wedding with Sharon's extended family taking up the pulpit side. The bride's folks are MIA.

Sharon McGrath is present, however; I am clutching her hand in mine in the pew furthest from the Dawson family. She would be alone again in her grief if it wasn't for me. I checked in with her after I had gotten home from yoga. She picked me up, and we came together. Just the two of us.

Who am I to judge her family? The only times I concern myself with what makes a family tick are when I see abuse, neglect, or the refusal to allow a sick child the miracle of modern medicine. *Mrs. Strong can be a fearsome advocate*—that was written more than once on my performance appraisals. The revolving door of school principals had to write that occasionally, even before I was a mandatory reporter of abuse. They would profusely apologize and tell me that my nemesis in the school system, Superintendent Mary Meade, made them issue the thinly veiled warnings. I count many friends and only a few enemies in this town, Mary Meade being one of the latter but every child that came through my classroom knew I had their back.

Today, I am here for two of my students. One is sitting next to me, and the other is dead.

Sharon has a different black dress today, one that fits her better. Her hair is flawless, and her make-up hasn't felt the sting of tears yet. That will come at the interment, I am sure.

The groomsmen are interspersed in the crowd with their families. The Reverend's daughter Rebecca, or Becky as she prefers to be called, was to be the maid of honor. She sits with her mother and brothers in their usual spot. Jake's sisters were to be Sharon's only bridesmaids. They are up front.

I tune out what is being said as I gaze about. The church is nearly filled, better than most Sundays, I imagine. I'm sure that Jeremiah takes weddings, baptisms, and funerals as an opportunity to reacquaint town folk with his ministry. Maybe he'll get more congregants from this crowd, but I doubt it. A senseless death by suicide doesn't impress me as a Come to Jesus moment, but I could be wrong.

Jeremiah is winding down. "He is no longer in pain and is in a better place." The sobbing increases. It pulls on my tear ducts. "He is with his Grandpa Jake, for whom he was named, and his Grandma Helen. May he rest in eternal peace."

Others get up to remember Jake. His auto body shop teacher and his oldest brother are the last to offer kind words. To a person, they describe his death as a surprise and a shock, no warning. "He had so much to live for. He had a bright future. He was always happy," ring in my ears repeatedly.

Barney Williams isn't here. He may show up at the gravesite, but probably not. He is the senior police officer in town. We have two full-timers and two part-timers. Major crimes or a fatal car wreck are handled by the State Police. I honestly don't know where a death by suicide fits in.

The speakers only validate what I already believe. I listen intently and I make a mental note to ask follow-up questions when I see them afterwards at the Dawson house.

The organist plays a hymn from the dog-eared hymnals. Those who know the song are too saddened to sing it well, and those who don't know the tune or for whom nineteenth-century songs of worship are a foreign language struggle with it respectfully in softer voices. Four verses later, the service mercifully ends.

Reverend Steele offers the benediction. The white-gloved pallbearers, whom I conclude were to be Jake's groomsmen, take positions around the casket. The organist plays the final dirge. Brian Yelito, his best man, is on the left front handle. They hoist the casket up. His face says it all. Tear-streaked cheeks, down-turned eyes, and a teeth-grinding set chin. This is what gut-wrenching pain and stoicism look like. Is that the face of a cold-blooded killer? What if it was a crime of passion done in the white-hot heat of the moment? How does a twenty-something hide it from all the people looking at him right now that he killed his best friend and business partner? Is he enough of a sociopath to pull this off?

I follow Brian through the sea of heads and shoulders until he is at the end of our pew. I just don't know. Maybe if I played poker all my life instead of teaching kindergarten, I would recognize a tell.

I watch closely as immediate family, extended family, friends, associates, and townsfolk make their way down the aisle. Sharon reminds me by squeezing my hand tightly that three days earlier, she was supposed to be walking down this same aisle with her husband, arm-in-arm. Now she's watching him carried away in a box. Her head hits my shoulder, and we hug tightly.

Right then, I decide to put her in the category of a witness and remove her as a suspect. Her other classmates who trail by us, I am not ready to peg so determinedly.

Sharon stays at the gravesite until everyone departs. She wants private time with the love of her life. Nobody knew her better than Jake, and they still have a lot to discuss. She assures me she will call me later to tell me she is okay. I will wait until tomorrow to ask if we can meet. We will have a lot to talk about, especially when she finds out that I don't think Jake's death was self-inflicted and that I am going to look into it.

I catch a ride with Emelina to the Dawson family home for the funeral reception.

She says, "My plate of chocolate chip cookies will yield me a return of foil-wrapped dinners that will last me a week. Funerals are a big deal when you are one of the oldest persons in town. Besides, the bereaved have enough food to feed an army. They are glad to give away some of the potluck. It's easier than trying to freeze it or throw it away."

"This is what I have to look forward to?" I ask. "Funerals and upgrading at potlucks?"

"Have you ever tried my chocolate chip cookies? People fight over them at the St. Paul's Holiday Bazaar. I would call it an even trade."

I reach into the back seat and pull one from underneath the plastic wrap. Whether it's because I am starved or because of the taste from only one bite, I find out why they are worth fighting over. I ask her with a mouthful of deliciousness, "Oh my God, this is so yummy. How do you do that?"

"It's a secret passed down by my great grandmother. I use butter. Lots of butter."

"Can I take a couple for Ken?"

"Be my guest."

I pull a handful of Dunkin' Donut napkins from her passenger door side pocket, carefully wrap two cookies, and slide them into my purse.

We park on a side road at the first available spot. I carry the cookies to the driveway. The house is average by Milford standards, but Warren built a free-standing three-car garage with a second story converted to the same number of bedrooms. The house is connected to the garage by a breezeway with a large screened-in porch. Emelina takes the prized chocolate chip cookies from me, and for a moment I feel empty-handed, but I get over it quickly as I realize seventy consecutive years of kindergarten teaching are approaching the front door. That's a lot of runny noses and untied shoes of Milford's citizenry.

Candace, the oldest daughter, greets us at the door. "Mrs. Bidwell, Mrs. Strong, thank you so much for coming."

"These are for your family, dear." Emelina hands her the platter.

"Are these your chocolate chip cookies?" Candace asks.

"Yes, dear." Emelina is beaming.

Candace winks. "I'll find a special hiding place for them." They depart to the kitchen.

Becky Steele greets me. "Hi, Mrs. Strong. I saw you with

Sharon in church and at the gravesite. How is she doing? It must be really tough for her."

I'm about to go into automatic response mode like I did at the viewing, but I stop myself. I take a deep breath. It's now or never. "How so?" I ask.

She's taken aback by my bluntness and looks from side to side before answering *sotto voce*. "Jake killed himself rather than get married to her. What does that tell you?"

I raise my eyebrows to that response and even more quietly ask her, "More importantly, what did she tell you, her maid of honor?"

"I was too freaked out about it all. Don't tell my mom and dad, but I had a little too much to drink at the rehearsal dinner, and when I realized he killed himself, I got hysterical."

"I'm sorry to hear that, Becky, but what did Sharon tell you?"

Becky looks at me with a screwed-up face in confusion. "Like I said, I was hysterical."

"Have you talked to her since you found out? I saw Sharon at the viewing, and she was completely alone."

"Mrs. Strong, I don't know what to tell you. Jake died. There is no wedding. I asked you how Sharon was doing, and you're playing twenty questions with me." Volume-wise, she goes from zero to sixty before bursting into tears and rushing off. What I saw was a flash of anger before her voice rose. It's not as if I hadn't seen five-year-olds throwing tantrums before.

Yvette Strohmeyer rushes over to me, "What was that about?"

"Becky Steele was to be Sharon's maid of honor, and she's asking me how Sharon is doing."

"I saw you at the viewing comforting Sharon and today at the service. It would be a reasonable question," Yvette shrugs.

"I didn't see Becky at the viewing."

"Neither did I," Yvette replies.

"Tell me, Yvette, a girl's best friend is asking their kindergarten teacher how the girl is doing after something terrible happens. Teachers are always the last people to find out what's going on." I raise my hands in an empty-handed gesture.

"Jake's death came as a shock to everybody," she replies. "People react differently. Maybe Becky is going through her own stuff. Besides, Mrs. Strong, Becky is a pastor's kid. Ask your own kids what's it like being a teacher's kid in the same school, what it's like always swimming in the fishbowl of a small town."

I nod my head. "I know what it's like being the only guppy in the goldfish bowl." Growing up a scared mixed-race child of a divorced white serviceman on a Royal Air Force base in rural England during the 1970s was a fishbowl all right.

I look down at Yvette's belly, as much in thought about Merry Olde England as the obvious change of subject question.

"Doc Lockhart says I am doing fine, and no, I haven't taken your pepperoni pizza advice, but if they have any here…"

"I guess I can cut Becky some slack, given the circumstances, but I think I will ask Sharon how they became besties."

Yvette smiles. "Look at you, Mrs. Strong sounding all hip."

I give her a hug. "Tru dat."

CHAPTER SEVEN

Ken wants to put a standing order in for Emelina's cookies. "You can't," I tell him. "She only bakes them for charity and to trade at potlucks."

"Ask her if she needs me to fix anything around her place. I'll make a sign," he says. "*Will work for chocolate chip cookies.*"

"I'll see her in the morning and ask her." The daily meditation and yoga are a perfect way to get over mourning not being in the classroom, and I want to make it a habit.

We are on the screened-in porch. He re-tacked the mesh screens, and we light citronella candles for the soft lighting as much as insurance against the maddening mosquitos. I say, "Yvette Strohmeyer said something to me at the funeral reception that got me thinking."

"She's way overdue, isn't she?" he asks.

I shake my head. "Doc Lockhart says she's doing fine. How do you think Erin and Wes grew up in my shadow as a teacher at Milford Elementary?"

"Can't say how it affected them. They turned out okay. I'd bet that Erin home-schooling the kids might have something to do with you being her teacher and always being around until eighth grade."

"What about Wes?"

It is my husband's turn to shake his head. "I think you have to ask him, Gwen. Going through school a few grades behind Erin made it harder for him. Why do you ask?"

"Yvette said Becky Steele grew up in a fishbowl because Jeremiah is a pastor of a church. She said our kids grew up with eyes on them because I was their teacher."

"I guess it would be the same as a cop's kid or the mayor's kid growing up in a small town," he says. "Might be tougher for Becky, though."

"How so?"

"It's one thing not to break the law. It's another to reflect badly on your dad when he preaches every Sunday. People would judge Jeremiah if she acted out."

We talk about some of the kids who have gone sideways. Almost without fail, it had to do with painkillers or heroin. He and I would be in the big box stores outside of town and get stopped by either somebody he worked for or a parent of a child I taught. They would tell us how everything was fine with their Jack or Jill when they went up the hill, but then we'd hear in painful detail how they came tumbling down.

Fights, thievery, cops, drug court, car wrecks, losing good jobs, probation, jail time, rehabs, twelve-step programs. In the beginning of their child's awful descent, the parents were like deer in the headlights—or full of denial. More often than not, we would hear how their teenager or young adult turned the parent's marriage upside down. Time away from work, drained life savings, even someone lifting a shirt in the paper goods aisle to show us an ugly bruise.

These folks sought a kind face. Who better than Ken, the friendly handyman, or Gwen, the kindergarten teacher? So, we both smiled and frowned at the right times. There wasn't much to say. These people didn't want our advice; they just wanted to be heard.

Then there were the folks who withdrew from life when their kids got addicted or into some other trouble. When they needed people to help share their burden, they turned inwards, and a few even turned suicidal. They needed as much help as their kids in figuring stuff out, but they were too ashamed to ask. We'd hear "everything is fine" or "life couldn't be better" followed by a tight smile in response to our genuine inquiry. Then they would avoid us in future encounters. There was no shortage of families ripped apart by drugs in our small town. We could have talked about them until midnight, but I had one last item on my agenda.

"Something else I want to talk to you about," I say.

Ken turns to me in the flickering candlelight.

"You might hear some things in the next couple of weeks about me." I take a deep breath, hold it for a second and let it whoosh out. "I've decided to look into Jake's death. I need convincing that he did that to himself."

"Okay, and…" he replies. I like when Ken asks me to explain things. It tells me he has his listening ears on.

"Before I do, I want to get Mabel and Warren's permission. I know I don't have to ask Sharon. The gossip mill says that Jake shot himself rather than get married to her. They were supposed to get hitched the following morning."

"Ouch."

"Yeah, tell me about it. If he did, then there has to be more to it," I say.

"But that's not exactly what you are telling me, is it, honey?" Sometimes he listens too well. It's time for me to come out of the shadows, to give myself permission to do this. I slide the candles closer to me to focus more light on the person who wants to do this.

"That's why I am giving you a heads up. I don't believe that he wanted to end his life. He had everything to live for. I think somebody else pulled the trigger, and I can figure it out."

He sits with that. It's not the first time we've talked about solving a murder. Last year, he met the FBI agent who asked for Erin and me to help. The shadows dance over his face. I watch as he weighs things out. Ken bobs his head back and forth like he's adding coins to a scale. Finally, he offers, "Why not? Is Erin going to help you?"

"I'm planning to run stuff by her and ask her what she thinks, but…"

"You want to figure it out mostly by yourself."

"Yep." The die is cast. I don't know how this is going to work. I wonder what the townsfolk are going to say when their favorite kindergarten teacher starts asking uncomfortable questions? I don't even have a lesson plan. All I know is that I have a burning desire to find out what happened.

"If it helps the Dawsons get closure, why not?" Ken's question is more of an affirmation.

"And Sharon too. Need to get rid of that awful stigma," I add.

"Go for it, Gwen." He rests a hand on my knee.

We blow out the candles and stand facing each other in the dark. The crickets are singing to us. The last of the lemony scent drifts away. My guy moves in and hugs me tightly. I don't care that he smells of sawdust and Old Spice. We kiss, and it's more than a comfortable peck. It doesn't take much to light my flame for him, and we wordlessly make our way upstairs.

CHAPTER EIGHT

"Mabel, I want to ask you something." It is the morning after the funeral. Her son has been in the ground for less than twenty-four hours. I thought about what I wanted to say to her all during my meditation and yoga earlier, but now I am tongue tied. "Do you still have questions about what happened to Jake?" I blurt out finally. We are seated on a bench outside of the newsstand in town. I asked her to meet me away from her home, as it was still probably filled with flower arrangements and other reminders.

"The shock is wearing off, Mrs. Strong, and I am still left with a ton of questions. Nothing can bring my son back, but I can't help but keep thinking he didn't do this to himself or to us."

"And Warren?"

"He's still devastated. It comes in waves for him. He can't work. He's taking more time off. His boss doesn't want him operating heavy equipment; told him to take as much time as he needs. He putters in the garage, then he rocks on the porch with a far-off look in his eyes. I have trouble reaching him."

"What's he thinking?"

Mabel takes a deep breath. "The police are ruling it a death by suicide. Warren doesn't like it but says they must have their reasons. They don't have to find out what caused Jake to do it, only that the evidence points to it being done by his own hand. We got a call from the coroner last night. Jake was drunk by driving standards, but barely—not enough to do anything stupid. There were no drugs in his system."

"How's that all sit with you, Mabel?" I ask gently.

"It doesn't. If he took a drug that he never took before or took too much of it, that would be one thing." She shakes her head and keeps tearing at the tissue balled in her fist. "It's like the police are doing half their job."

Now's not the time to tell her they didn't do a full toxicology screen. The light changes to green, and a logging truck grinds gears past us. I summon the courage to say, "I want to do the other half for you. I want to ask around, see what I can find out. There's more to this story, I know. The question is, do you want to learn what I discover? It could be more painful than not knowing the truth."

"I hadn't considered that, Gwen."

"There's something else to think about. He may not have done this to himself." I have to be careful talking with her. To me, this is a case I can nose around in. To her, I am talking about her baby boy.

"I've thought about that," she tells me. "Why would someone want to kill Jake? It makes no sense."

"If that is the case," I say.

"Then his killer is still out there. Oh, God," Mabel says.

"I'd be opening up a can of worms," I say.

"But we would know more than we do now, and that's not much, only that he ended his life." She sniffs and looks down at her hands. "Supposedly."

Traffic goes by; the wind rustles the trees; the mid-morning sun bathes half the street in bright sunlight while our side is left in shadow for now. I know that Mabel is considering the offer.

"I can't pay you," she says.

"I agree. Our state has strict licensing laws for private investigators. I'd be doing it as a favor."

"Why?"

"Because I have the time and because I can." I tell her the short version of what happened in New Haven.

Duly impressed, she says, "Gwen, I didn't know any of that."

"Does it surprise you?" I ask.

"Not at all." She smiles. "You read all my kids like a book. I was jealous when we'd talk in the store or out on the street about my bunch and you knew how they were doing or what they were doing better than me."

"Teachers can be one step ahead of a parent when they see the kids all day in school, especially in a small school like Milford Elementary. A lot of parents work and are exhausted at night."

"And still have to make dinner, supervise homework, and get them ready for bed," she adds.

"Exactly. School is a little more controlled setting, whereas home can be…"

"Nutso."

I nod. I lift a fresh familiar black and white spotted composition book from my tote, click my favorite pen, and say, "Let's start with the rehearsal dinner. Tell me all about it—and leave nothing out."

It's too nice to sit inside on a bright afternoon with low humidity and gentle breezes. It is a perfect day for a hike. I always said that when I gazed out the windows of my classroom on days like today. On some of those days, I would march my class on the sidewalks completely around the building, and we would serenade their envious schoolmates with a Mr. Rogers song.

By choice now though, I am staring out the window of Sharon's top-floor efficiency apartment. I can see the bench that Mabel and I sat on that very morning. Sharon lives in a converted attic in a large downtown Victorian. The ceiling is slanted over her bedroom. Her living area and kitchenette take up the front side of the house. She has two large monitors docked to her laptop. Her fingers fly on the wireless keyboard. She's bringing up the wedding reception guest list for me.

I told her what I wanted to do, and she hugged me fiercely. I had one condition. I might ask her questions and sometimes not be able to tell her why I was asking or to answer her questions. I promise her I will share everything I learn, regardless of what it is, when I finish or hit a dead end. She's okay with that. She wants to know about what happened as much as I do.

She works at home as a customer service rep for a software application, troubleshooting user problems. Today she is supposed to be on her honeymoon vacation. Instead, she spent the morning returning gifts to guests. She set them on each person's porch, rang the bell, and retreated to her car for her next stop. Trick or Treat in reverse.

The printer spits out the list. Names, addresses, and emails. Nice. Just to be safe, I ask her to email it to both Erin and me.

Contrasting the beautiful day is her dark mood. Sharon McGrath is not Mrs. Jake Dawson. The white skin her engagement ring covered for over a year on her finger marks her as single, but not widowed. Guys will hit on her thinking she's a young divorcee.

"You know, Mrs. Strong, the cops never interviewed me. I wasn't even officially notified. I was not next of kin. In fourteen hours, we were to be married, but until then, I was just his girlfriend."

"Did you live with him?" I ask.

"Call us old-fashioned. I was going to move stuff over gradually after we came home from the honeymoon. I had this apartment 'til the end of September. Mrs. Laski says I can stay now on a month-to-month lease."

"She's very kind," I say.

"We were going to go shopping for a queen bed when we got back from the honeymoon. He is still using the bed from his childhood bedroom. The pillowcases and bedcovers have race car designs. 'Zoom, Zoom,' he would say." Sharon clutches her shoulders with both hands. She misses the memory of his touch.

"How did you find out?"

"Mrs. Dawson called my parents. Then they called me."

"When was that?"

"Two thirty-three in the morning. I don't know why I had the phone on ringer that night. My world changed forever in that moment. They woke me from a light sleep. I couldn't believe it. I thought it was a cruel wedding prank at first. Then it hit me. I drove over to my folks' house in a daze."

I can see her eyes on me as I stare at what I wrote in my notebook.

"What are you thinking, Mrs. Strong?" she asks.

"What exactly do you remember them telling you?"

"Jake was dead, that he shot himself."

"Did they say when?"

"No, but later, I learned it was around midnight."

"Do you remember who told you?"

"Brian. Brian Yelito."

"How did he find out?"

Sharon shrugs her shoulders. I make a note to ask Brian myself.

"I remember you telling me that at the viewing," I continue. "The police were calling it a death by suicide in less than two hours of investigation. They wouldn't even have an analysis for GSR that fast."

"GSR?"

"Gunshot residue. I'm sorry, Erin could explain it better, but when you shoot a gun, gases and particles from the shell push the bullet down the barrel. They escape the gun and can land on the shooting hand. They have a couple of tests for that. They are pretty accurate."

Sharon stares at me dumbfounded.

"My daughter Erin is a true-crime junkie. That's all she talks about when she isn't telling me about my precious grandchildren. We went on a mother-daughter weekend last year to a symposium on this stuff. It was fascinating. She tells me about the latest cases she watches on cable and how they get solved. I am learning so much from her."

"It makes sense," she says.

"What do you mean?"

"You always wanted to know what happened back in school."

"You remember that about me?" I ask.

She nods. "If there was a fight on the playground and nobody was talking about who started it, you always figured it out."

"Is that true?" I am surprised by these observations.

She nods again. "Everybody knew not to lie to Mrs. Strong."

"I'll have to ask Ken and the kids what it was like living with an amateur sleuth." I try to laugh it off.

Sharon doesn't brush off my aside. "It's true. Watch and see," she says. "That's why I think you are the perfect person to help Jake."

This angle had dawned on me. If he was murdered, I'd be helping find his murderer. It would give my dead student closure.

She gives me the gospel according to Sharon on all the rehearsal dinner guests and the closest people in Jake's world who were invited to the wedding. I devoted a page to each person and quickly make an index page at the end of the notebook of all their names alphabetically. I can see myself flipping pages endlessly if I didn't do that. I need to develop a timeline, too. Erin could help me with that.

The afternoon flies by. Shadows have lengthened across the street. I ask Sharon if she has keys to Jake's cabin. She does. I call Mabel and Erin in quick succession.

"A couple more things about the business. Candace was the body shop's bookkeeper. They didn't have payroll since it was just Jake and Brian. She would prepare the quarterly estimates for the CPA to file and help them tie out the books at year's end."

"Who is that?"

"Bo Sager."

"Oh, he's Ken's CPA too," I say.

"Jake complained that she was always on him about expenses and that he didn't charge enough."

"Isn't a lot of that controlled by what the insurance companies will pay?"

"Yes, but that brings me to the other thing. They had a huge customer for Mustang re-builds. The Stillman brothers would find Mustangs all over the area, then bring them to Jake and Brian. The boys would fix them up, and the brothers would ship them to buyers all over the country. Candace figured out that the boys could charge way more than insurance rates for the parts and labor."

"Simon and Jason, they are twins, aren't they?" I ask.

"Yes."

"Their family moved into town when they were in high school, I believe."

"Older than me and Jake by about five years," she says

"They went through high school between Erin and Wes, I think."

Sharon says, "That sounds about right."

"What do they do for a living?" I ask.

"I asked Jake that exact question and he said, 'Don't ask.' He told me they drive around in shiny new trucks with fancy wheels all day."

"And?"

"That's it, they just drive around. When Jake pressed them on how they got their money, Simon, the smart one, said they have several internet marketing businesses. The Mustangs don't pay enough for them to be driving those kinds of wheels."

"Hmmm." I leave a comfortable silence for Sharon to fill.

"They dealt mostly with Brian, and he and Jake had an argument about inviting them to the wedding. Since my folks were paying the lion's share of the reception costs, Jake told Brian they couldn't come."

"I see." I write on Brian's page, *Brian-Stillman twins-Mustangs? Brian-time of death?* I glance at my watch. Still time for one last lead. "Sharon, we got off to a good start here. I have lots to work with. Can I text you if I have a quick question?"

She lifts her phone, thumbs a few keys in a blur, then my phone buzzes. I read, *Yes, you can any time day or night. Thanks for everything.* We stand, hug automatically, and then hug again.

Perfect timing. I step into the turn of the century Borough Hall after the front desk secretary has gone home, but before Barney Williams leaves to direct traffic. I hear his booming laugh across the room. The Looney Tunes cartoon character Foghorn Leghorn comes to mind whenever I hear his voice. Now imagine that rooster in a police uniform.

Barney bounces up to the counter with a swagger and strut. "Hello, Mrs. Strong. Come to pay a parking ticket?"

I taught this man. How that mischievous miscreant became a police officer is beyond me.

"Hello, Barney. I would like a copy of the police report on Jake Dawson's death last Friday night."

"Why, Mrs. Strong? It was ruled a death by suicide by the coroner."

"Thank you for telling me it's a closed file. In that case, I'd like the 911 calls, the CAD report, and the scene photos as well." I smile.

"Well, I can't do that," he stutters.

"Sure, you can, Barney."

"No, I mean I don't have the calls and photos. That is done by the State Police. How do you know about CAD reports?"

"Computer Assisted Dispatch logs all calls and dispatches, right? I want them too."

Flustered, he says, "I know what they are. The Stateys have them too."

"Okay, I'll take the Milford Police reports on the response."

"Why?"

"Why what, Barney?"

"Why do you want them?" He narrows his squint at me while setting his cap on the table. Traffic is going to back up a bit today, I am afraid.

"Barney," I say, shaking my head, "you know as well as I do that, I do not have to supply a reason."

"Are you making a Freedom of Information request?"

"It will take longer to discuss it then it would to open that filing cabinet, pull out the file and make the copies, Barney." I treat him like a schoolchild, a petulant schoolchild with a badge and a gun.

Barney is not normally a bully, but today, he throws his sizable girth around. "You will need to make a written request.

Now, if you'll excuse me." He starts towards the swing gate to the side of the counter.

I block his move. "I thought you might say that, Officer Williams." I pull out my composition notebook, open a fresh page, then click my pen and do exactly as he requested. He is trapped behind the gate, lest he decide to steamroll his former kindergarten teacher. I carefully remove the page and hand it to him across the gate. "Here you go, Barney. I'll pick it up tomorrow. Be careful not to redact anything I am entitled to."

CHAPTER NINE

I open the front door of Jake's cabin with Sharon's key, and we get hit in the face with a blast of putrid air.

"It smells like death," Erin says as I close the door swiftly.

"I don't disagree with you." We stand frozen, almost like thieves debating whether to trespass.

"Are you prepared for what we might see?" she asks.

"I don't know what to expect other than Mabel telling me that nobody has come here to clean up yet. So, not really, but we are here, and it's still daylight." If I were alone, I might turn back, but I asked Erin to accompany me. She had a quick dinner on the table for when her husband, Darren, walked in, then she drove straight to Milford, telling him she was working on a murder investigation with his favorite mother-in-law.

We are hit with the stench again as I reopen the door. Will we ever get this odor out of our clothes? I regret wearing one of my better outfits. We take a step inside and see the source. Congealed blood on the dining table and floor gives off a sickening, sweet metallic scent. It is spattered along the wall and window as well.

"Would've been nice to have the scene photos," she says.

"We will just have to take our own," I reply.

Beer cans sit on end tables. A pizza box contains one last piece and several crusts. Plates and bowls rest in the drying rack next to the sink in the small kitchen. I notice a few goose feathers on the floor, but otherwise the wooden floors are clean. Dusty, but clean. I see a rehearsal dinner after-party with the guys for one last hurrah.

"Jake didn't get around to tidying up before pulling the trigger would be the assumption," she says.

"If you were to believe he did this to himself," I complete her sentence. "Something else interrupted his revelry is my best guess."

Erin lifts her phone and videos the interior of the cabin. She gives the time and date and location. She moves through the dining area, to the kitchen, then turns left into a doorway, and a few seconds reappears from another doorway, completing her video tour.

"The kitchen has a doorway to the bathroom, and the bathroom has a door to the bedroom," she says for me and for the recording before shutting off the video.

She then takes photos as we move closer to the dining table. It is a small hand-me-down with a setting for two. The chairs are mismatched. Blood has dripped off the table into a puddle on the floor. The spray pattern of blood several feet away fans out on the closed window, sill, and wall on the same side of the table as the puddle. I tap the flashlight app on my phone and shine it on the wall to better illuminate the scene for Erin's photography.

Erin points. "He was probably sitting down in the chair facing the kitchen when he was shot, and his head came to rest on the table."

"The blood then ran off the table onto the floor," I add.

"With the blood spatter against that wall—" she starts.

"I wouldn't be surprised if the fatal head wound was on the left side of his head," I finish her out loud thought.

"One would be led to believe that he shot himself with his left hand," she concludes. The two of us work well together.

"I can't remember from school or from when he completed the estimate for my father's car what hand he uses," I say. I text Sharon: *Was Jake left-handed?*

No? comes the reply. *Why?* comes the obvious question.

Won't know until I look at the autopsy report, I answer.

"Shot himself with his off hand, hmm? Makes me wonder," Erin says.

"Me too."

"Wonder what kind of gun was used."

"Why?"

"With a revolver, the spent shell would stay in the chamber. With an automatic pistol, the shell would be ejected."

I take only a few seconds to realize where the shell would have been ejected to. We both look back towards the doorway.

"If it was a pistol, they should have taken a photo of the shell on the ground," I say hopefully.

"If it was, and they didn't, then we can assume they had this written off as a death by suicide from the get-go," Erin replies.

We drift from the dining area along the right wall to the kitchen and the rear of the square-shaped cabin. I put on a dishwashing glove and open the fridge. The guy cooked for himself. I open the freezer. Not much. He went from week to week. Erin takes photos of both openings. In another week or less, this stuff will be removed. We repeat the process with the tabletops and cabinets. Who knows if we will ever need these photos? But it is better to have them?

Next is the bathroom. I go right to the medicine cabinet and see that there are no meds in there. "I'll get Mabel to sign an authorization to allow me to get Jake's medical records and pharmacy orders."

"But there is nothing in there," she says after taking photos of the toiletries.

"What if someone took them?"

"That's what Casey or Marsha would ask." Erin smiles. She is referring to New Haven Police Detective Casey McFadden and FBI agent Marsha O'Shea, whom we worked with last year.

"The absence of something gives us clues, Erin," I tell her.

She beams. "Spoken like a true sleuth."

We move to the bedroom. *Zoom! Zoom!* I tell Erin, "Sharon told me that this was Jake's childhood bed, and that after the honeymoon they were going to get a queen-size." The cartoon designs of NASCAR cars with numbers on the doors flying around the racecourse works well with the checkered flags.

I open the bedstand and blush. I am standing next to my daughter as we both look at a collection of sex toys and lubes.

"That looks like the newer model," Erin says nonchalantly as she takes a few shots.

"Erin!" I feel like such a voyeur.

"What?"

"Those weren't part of the birds and bees talk, honey."

She eyerolls me. "Oh, Mom."

We move to the dresser, and like good burglars, we open the bottom first and move up.

In the top drawer of his dresser, we spot a clip of ammunition.

Erin slips on my other glove and retrieves it. "It's for an eight shot. .45-caliber. He has a cleaning kit for it too." She puts the clip back after taking a photo of it on top of the bed.

We both look under the bed. There is no boogeyman, but there are cases for two long guns. I push the dust bunnies aside and find a double-barreled shotgun and a scoped deer rifle, both with ammo.

"Hunting and self-defense will be added to my questions," I

say. I zip up the cases, then put them back under the bed and gaze about the room.

"Something doesn't feel right, Erin. I just can't put my finger on it." We stand in silence. "This room is speaking to me, but—"

"Guns and ammunition?"

"No, something else." We stand and listen inwardly.

"Look at the photos tomorrow. Maybe it will jog your memory, Mom."

"Good idea."

We move to the living area to the left of the dining area. A threadbare couch, a coffee table, and an easy chair are angled towards a TV and a video game console on the floor in front of it. They are both next to the bedroom wall. We pull the cushions off just like they do in the movies, but there are no hidden clues. Somehow, we've gotten accustomed to the smell, but I am sure our spouses won't be so happy when we get home.

"Let's walk the perimeter before it gets dark," Erin suggests.

The cabin is nestled along the mountain and state game lands on the edge of town. Jake could walk out his backyard and into legal hunting woodlands for a mile in either direction. We dip into the tree line to look for any signs that someone had watched his cabin. We photograph the cabin from each side while searching for anything that looks suspicious. The sun is now down over the mountain and is throwing the small plot of land and gravel driveway into deep cool shade. I make sure all the doors are locked and leave the windows the way they were.

Sitting in Erin's car, we stare at the cabin as dusk settles in.

"Can't wait to see the crime scene photos," Erin says. "I did the FOI request with the State Police the minute I hung up with you."

"After yoga tomorrow, I plan to pay a visit to Officer Barney Williams again. I want his report before I talk to other people," I reply.

"He was a few years behind me in school, but ahead of Wes. Never thought in a million years he'd become a cop."

"He wouldn't be my first choice to give a loaded weapon to," I say.

"Most likely the State Police will have the full coroner's report," she tells me, then we crunch gravel as we leave the driveway.

In a New York minute, we decide the next course of action is to get the police reports before taking another step. If they stonewall us, I will interview persons furthest away from Jake in relationship first. I don't want to talk to his closest associates until I see those reports.

"Did you have dinner?" I ask.

"Just a couple of protein bars," she says.

"Want me to have your father throw on another chicken breast? He's grilling tonight."

"Sure, Mom, but…"

"What?" I ask.

"Our clothes."

"Oh, right, we can put them in the wash. I am sure I have something that will fit you."

"That will work."

"What else, baby?" I sense when my daughter has something on her mind.

"We just worked a murder scene, didn't we, Mommy?"

"Feels that way, doesn't it?"

CHAPTER TEN

I am in a serene place after yoga. I wrestled with the crime scene in my mind all during meditation but breathing through all those sun salutations allowed me to just pay attention to my body and the pouring out of yesterday's stress. Abe used the Sanskrit word for corpse pose once before. Laying on the floor, legs slightly splayed and listening to his soothing voice, knocks me out. I awake (for the third time in this house in a week) feeling rested, alert, and closer to getting the answer that Jake's bedroom was trying to tell me. It will come to me, I am sure.

I see two State Police cruisers in the Borough Hall parking lot, which is next to the courthouse. It's not uncommon to see them there. Our little town, wedged between a mountain and a river, is also the county seat. I walk up the steps and pull on the heavy oak door.

Vickie, the Borough secretary, is seated at her desk gazing at her flat screen monitor. She smiles and then frowns when she recognizes me and tries to avert her eyes.

"Hey, Vickie. How are you?" I taught this girl not more than a dozen years earlier. She is the mayor's youngest daughter.

"I am doing well, Mrs. Strong." She appears nervous and tries tapping a few keys to make it as if there is something more important than Instagram cat reels on her screen.

"Still going to the community college?"

"Taking just a couple of night classes this semester." She's not making eye contact with me.

"The credits add up, Vickie." I try to sound hopeful, but I suspect that this is her way of slowly convincing her parents that more schooling is not for her. She did just enough to get by and fly below the radar throughout eight grades, then I heard nothing otherwise about her at the regional high school. What was that thing that Ken and I talked about the other night about kids swimming in a fishbowl?

She looks up at my smiling face and then over her shoulder. She whispers to me, "They are talking about you in there. What did you do?"

I am taken aback. I sputter, "Nothing criminal, but I hoped that you would have a police report for me on the Jake Dawson death by suicide from last Friday night."

"That's what it's about then. They've been in there for the last half-hour talking about something. They told me that if you came in to tell you that the case is reopened and you aren't allowed to have the report."

Her words punch me in the gut. The wind leaves my diaphragm, and I cannot speak for a moment. What happened overnight that would cause them to reopen the investigation? I am betting it is two words—Gwendolyn Strong.

I rest my hand on the counter until I stop seeing stars, only to open them and see the bewildered look on her face. "Are you okay? Mrs. Strong?"

It is as if the last two glorious hours of meditation and yoga never happened. What do they call the term? Fight or flight? I see Mabel, Warren, and Jake Dawson in my mind's eye. I remember the hugs with Sharon McGrath. I had to learn to fight for myself when I was a kid. I never backed down then. I will not run away now.

"Please tell Officer Williams that I would like to see him."

Vickie looks like she doesn't want to be the ping-pong ball in this match of wills. "Okay, I will do that for you, Mrs. Strong."

She gets up and knocks on the door of the office, then is ushered in. I stare at the door until it opens slightly and see Moe, Larry, and Curly staring back at me. The door closes quickly, and more hushed tones slip under the one-inch gap at the bottom. I know Ken didn't hang that door.

Eventually, she returns red-faced with downcast eyes. "I'm sorry, Mrs. Strong. Officer Williams is busy in a meeting with the State Police." She talks as she walks back to her chair and makes it obvious in the way she collapses into it that she is not getting back up.

"Thank you, Vickie. Please tell them I will wait here." Louder I say, "They can't hide behind that door forever."

She reaches for her phone just as the door opens, then the angry-looking police officer I know motions me forward.

The crowded office contains three seated law enforcement officers, two in uniform and one in a well-tailored suit. His shoulder holster is a giveaway. His short black hair is cut military-style; he is squared jawed and clean-shaven. Slightly older than Barney, but trim and athletic, he speaks without introduction and with none of them offering me a seat. "What is your interest in Jake Dawson's death by suicide, Mrs. Strong?"

"As of five o'clock last night, it was closed with the coroner finding it as such. When did that change?"

"Who is Erin LeGrande, Mrs. Strong?"

Of course, he would ask about Erin. This guy is good.

I answer his question with a question. "More importantly, what is the status of her FOI request?"

"According to witnesses, you were tampering with a crime

scene last evening before dark. What do you have to say about that?" We are playing hardball.

"I seem to be at a loss here. Who am I speaking with, and why hasn't one of you offered me a seat?"

He doesn't move, but Barney jumps up, scoots his chair around the desk, and stands against the far wall. "Thank you, Barney," I say. "You always had good manners in school." I sit down and then pull the chair close to where my knees are nearly touching my accuser's. "Let's get off on the right foot. You are not talking to some scared teenager blinded by a flashlight beam in their face on a lonely stretch of interstate. You know my name, and you know darn well that Erin is my daughter, because she went to Milford Elementary around the same time as Barney. As far as tampering with a crime scene, I hope you don't play poker and try to bluff when you have nothing in your hand."

The man smiles. "Detective James Shafer, and you are right. I don't play poker very well. Yes, I became involved after your visit to Officer Williams last night and when we received your daughter's request. The investigation has been reopened, uh, for my review. My superiors would like me to go over it, but," he stops to look at the other two men in the claustrophobic setting, "I'm not sure why. Mr. Dawson had GSR on his hand, and there was stippling against his temple."

I narrow my eyes, cock my head, and ask evenly, "Motive?"

He clears his throat and looks at the others. "We don't need to show motive."

"That's true for most crimes, including homicide," I say, "but death by suicide always includes looking for motive. You always look for a note. There was no note." It's my turn to shade the truth. I don't know this for 100 percent.

"How do you know that?" he asks. This time, he is polite.

"The parents would have been told when they were notified." I count on my index finger. I look at Barney. "Two," I add my middle finger, "the people that transported him would have said something. After all, we are a small town. And three," I add my ring finger, "the coroner would have mentioned it when the toxicology report findings were released to the family." I smile plainly.

"Okay," he says. "Let's agree there is no note."

He says that too quickly, and I make a mental note of how he says it. "One thing is bugging me though." I push the chair back and stand.

I wait until he asks, "What's that, Mrs. Strong?"

"Why did he shoot himself with his non-dominant hand?"

I can tell by their furtive glances that the trained law enforcers hadn't asked themselves that question.

"Mrs. Strong, how do you know that?" Shafer asks.

I smile. "I'll point out how when you and I go over the crime scene photos, Detective."

He cranes his head to look around me. "This woman was your kindergarten teacher, Barney?" Shafer shakes his head at me. "Sorry, no can do. Like we said, the investigation is reopened."

"Please keep one thing in mind as you go about your investigation, Detective Shafer," I say. "Jake Dawson died the night before his wedding precisely because his life would change the next day. Figure what that change was, and you will find how why he died." I look down on him, then over to his two meek companions. "May I have your card?"

He reaches into his credentials and pulls out a crisp one, handing it to me.

"You know how to reach me from both our FOI requests."

I end the meeting with a swoosh out the door.

I smile at Vickie. "Good luck in school, Vickie. Say hello to your mom and dad for me." My head is throbbing. Is this what a migraine feels like?

I walk quickly past the cruisers. My vision narrows. There is an aura surrounding what I see. I try to breathe deep, but I can't. I am reduced to panting open mouthed like the time I ran a 5K on a muggy day and did not train for it. I shuffle down the sidewalk between the courthouse and Borough Hall to the rear alley where the trash bins are kept. I lurch around the corner, then pull on my last bit of energy to push myself behind a dumpster. I throw up.

CHAPTER ELEVEN

"I thought that was you." I hear the shrill voice of Mary Meade. "Looking for recyclables now that you are retired, Gwen?"

I am still bent over and barely aware of her voice as the stars in my eyes clear. Not now, Mary, not now. Pretending to be looking for something, I move further away from her prying eyes.

"Shhh," I say. I keep low, shielded by the dumpster. Ken is going to wonder why my clothes smell horrible every time I come home. But I've got to do something here.

"Here kitty, kitty. Here kitty, kitty." I keep ignoring Mary until I can stand up straight, then I emerge from the other side of the dumpster.

"Did you see a black kitten, Mary?" I ask before disappearing behind the other dumper.

I can tell she is dubious of my stated purpose by her drippy reply. "No, I didn't."

"I thought I heard a faint mewing. Here kitty, kitty." I am further away from her when I reach the sidewalk.

"Always a protector of small animals," she says with a smirk. I am reminded of the time one of my pupils found a robin's nest with babies that my class nursed to health. Or was it the tiny rabbits?

"Sorry, Mary," I say, "no time to chat. I'm on my way to the coroner's office." How I enjoy getting the last word in with her.

I walk less like the walking dead with each stride as I make my way to Tom Cleary's office. Dark clouds have rolled in, and I'll need to get home before it pours. His office is at the other funeral home in town several blocks away. I need this walk to clear my brain.

At least I didn't puke in front of the officers. I wasn't expecting to be ambushed. That was the first time a police officer ever threatened me with arrest. I am sure that is what I reacted to. This must be the price for standing up to bullies when you can't use your fists.

Detective Shafer had given two important facts though: Jake had gunshot residue on his hand, and the gun was close enough to the side of his head to cause other marks besides the bullet's entry wound. I am less inclined to think of his death as a murder, but the police still don't have a motive. Am I slow to change my opinion, or is something still nagging at me? What was that about agreeing with me that there was no note?

At least they can't keep me from seeing the coroner's report. By doing so, I am choosing to honor my decision to seek closure for the Dawsons and Sharon. Was it my father or my husband who said I am stubborn? Probably both.

"I must charge you for the report, Mrs. Strong. The toxicology report is extra," Tom tells me.

He is a stoop-shouldered older man with a sallow face and pasty gray hair. I wonder if embalming fluid has seeped into his system over the years. He is widowed and didn't have any kids in the school system, but I have seen him many times at charity functions. "You can get it from the police as part of their investigation for the cost of photocopies," he offers.

I could if it was a closed case. "Can you tell me your findings?"

"Why? The boy shot himself."

"Has anybody given you a motive?" He shakes his head. "How much are the reports?"

"This is highly irregular, Mrs. Strong. We normally make copies for the police. But for the insurance companies and probate lawyers, it is $400 for the full report and $100 for the tox scan."

"I don't have $500 to give you, Tom."

"Then you should get a copy from the police." He starts to put the report back in the filing cabinet.

"I can't."

"Why's that?"

"They decided to reopen the investigation."

"They what? When?"

"This morning. After I made a request for the file from Barney Williams last night, and after my daughter made a similar request of the State Police, they decided to reopen it." I shrug.

"Do they have anything to tell them this wasn't death by suicide?" he asks.

"No."

"I don't understand."

"By reopening the investigation, they don't have to give me copies of anything under Freedom of Information."

"Is that so?"

"I am sad to say so, Tom. I promised Mabel and Warren—"

"The boy's parents?"

"Yes."

We stand in silence. He slowly shuffles over to his desk and looks in his empty blue Yale Med School coffee mug. He takes the file and opens it on the counter. "May I borrow your phone?"

"What?"

"May I borrow your phone? I'd like to make a call upstairs while I fetch another cup of coffee."

Tom leaves me with my composition notebook and the file for the time it takes to make slow-drip coffee. He took my phone so I can't take photos of his file.

I hurry through the report. Erin was right. They only tested for alcohol and the usual drugs. No PCP or angel dust, mushrooms, or designer psychedelics. Cause and manner of death are consistent with a self-inflicted gunshot to the left side of the head. They swabbed for nitrates on his left hand, and it came up positive. The slug was sent to the State Police lab. There are no defensive wounds or marks anywhere on his body. There is nothing remarkable in his autopsy.

I hear footsteps on the stairs. I glance at the autopsy photos and start to get a sick feeling in my stomach again. The last photo was taken at the scene. It confirms the position of the body, just as Erin and I imagined it was.

Tom steps back into the room. "Thank you for letting me use your phone, Mrs. Strong. Cell reception is so much better upstairs."

I close the file and tuck my notebook back into my bag. "Glad I could help."

We smile as I quickly depart. It is raining, but I see some sun shining through on this case.

∼

My phone rings as I hit the pavement. It is from a number I don't recognize. I answer. "Hello?"

"Hi, Mrs. Strong, this is Candace, Mabel's oldest. We met last week."

I duck under an elm tree. Nature's umbrella. "Yes, I remember. How can I help you?"

"Mom told me you are looking into what happened to Jake."

"Yes, Sharon told me you are the boys' bookkeeper. I was hoping to talk to you too."

"That's what I am calling about. I have some information that I think you might be interested in."

"I'm downtown. When can we meet?"

"I work at Emory's Auto Parts. We can talk during my lunch break."

I glance at my watch. "Do you want me to grab you a sandwich?"

"No thank you, I brown bagged it today."

"See you at noon?"

"Yes, that works perfectly."

I grab a pre-made chicken salad, chips, and a large, sweet tea at the Quickie-Mart. It's only a block over to Emory's, and I do a fair job of walking under awnings and dodging raindrops to stay dry.

When I arrive, I am waved into the office by the counter person. Boxes of inventory overstock and returns line two cinderblock walls. An old green metal four drawer desk holds a monitor keyboard. Candace's lunch rest on deli paper next to a Mountain Dew.

Candace and I hug. It's natural. I taught all the kids, and Mabel told her I was working for them.

"I only have a half-hour," she tells me, "especially since I took the last two days off without pay. I can eat while we talk."

"They don't have a bereavement policy here?" I almost wish I could take that question back.

"If this were a chain store, yes, but this franchisee is very strict about time off. I used all my vacation time during the summer. I am not getting paid for the last two days." She shakes her head. "Rules are rules."

I set out my lunch and my notepad, then fork the salad and grab some chips.

"Did Sharon tell you about the Stillman twins?" she asks.

"A little. What do you know about them? I'd rather hear some stuff twice than assume I know the story."

"Jake and Brian did a lot of favors for the older folks in town. Get their business, then they'd tell their families. Some jobs never saw an insurance appraiser. Some customers didn't want to get cancelled or have their rates go up. They did those jobs at cost, and it worked. They became the go-to auto body shop in town. The bulk of the regular paying jobs were insurance claims and deer strikes. The insurance companies are sticklers and make sure they don't pay a penny more than they have to, and I am really talking about nickels and dimes. The boys did a nice volume, but both were working six and seven days a week. Banging fenders is difficult work." She takes a bite of her sandwich while I stab at my salad. Yesterday's chicken is today's chicken salad, I am reminded as I swallow.

She continues. "Their profit margin is razor thin for most jobs, break-even for some, and then there are the Stillman twins. Young guys acting like bigshots with their fancy trucks. They don't fool me."

"Oh?"

"They are doing something illegal. I just don't know what it is."

"Why do you say that?"

"Cash. Cash for everything. Cash at the body shop for all the Mustang restores. Cash here at this store. I even checked at the dealerships. Big cash down payments, and they use a casino pre-paid debit card for the monthly payments."

"Casino pre-paid debit card?"

"If you ever want to launder money, Mrs. Strong, take a wheelbarrow full of cash to the casino, and they will gladly set up an account for you to gamble, but you can also set up withdrawals on the card. It's untraceable. I could set up an account in Mickey Mouse's name, and as long as I know how to access it, nobody's the wiser."

"That's incredible," I say between bites.

"I'm thinking the Mustangs are a way for them to launder money, but I just can't figure it out."

"How do Jake and Brian fit into it?"

"Since the twins are doing something funky, I told them to charge more for their labor and the parts. These are 'restoration' builds. Jake and Brian were doing specialized work and had to spend more time finding the parts."

"And?"

"At first, Jake didn't want to take my advice, and Brian pushed back too, saying they were getting cash. They didn't have to report the jobs on their taxes."

"And what did you have to say?"

"I said an IRS auditor would look at all the Mustang parts and wonder what cars the guys were putting them on. I argued that the twins had a huge profit margin, and the guys doing the heavy lifting should get a slice of the pie."

"Makes sense to me."

"Brian said they would start paying cash for those parts and that nothing about the cars would go into the books. Jake was okay with that, but he didn't like dealing with the Stillmans. He would have been happy just playing by the rules."

"So, what happened?"

"Jake wouldn't touch the Mustangs. He wouldn't order parts or do the rebuilds or any of the painting. Told Brian he could keep all the money. When the Stillmans saw the slowdown, they confronted Jake, and he told them they could shove it. He didn't want their money. Brian smoothed things over by saying he was going to get some Vo-Tech seniors to work with him on the Mustangs over weekends to catch up. Great experience for them, cheap labor for Brian. And the Stillman Mustangs and their dirty cash were splitting up two lifelong friends," Candace concluded.

"Do you think that Jake knew where the Stillmans were getting their cash?" I ask.

"He said nothing to me. Did he tell Sharon about them?"

"Just a little, but nothing like what you told me today," I say. "Sharon sensed some unrest with Jake over the twins."

Candace glances at the clock, then scrunches up her deli paper into a ball and tosses it in the wastepaper basket in the corner. "Tell her that I don't think that Jake killed himself, and if he did, it wasn't over her. Those two were in love. They were soulmates, and I don't say that lightly. My family didn't know what to think when it happened. We treated her poorly. Please apologize on our behalf."

At that moment, Mr. Emory pops his head into the room. "Oh, hello, Mrs. Strong. I didn't know you had company, Candace." He glances at the clock before ducking back out again.

She shakes her head. "I watched my baby brother get buried about this time two days ago, and he's worried about me overextending my lunch period."

"Candace, I will keep asking questions until I get an answer."

"Thanks, I know you will."

We get up and hug again. I toss my trash, then walk out to the sidewalk. The rain is getting heavier, and I am not sure where I am going next.

Candace comes out behind me in a rush. "I almost forgot to tell you something that is very important. It's why I called you in the first place."

"What's that?"

"Brian and Jake went to some Small Business Administration meeting years ago on startups, and the presenters suggested that business partners take a life insurance policy out on each other, in case something happens. They've been paying those premiums for several years now."

My stomach flutters. I remember thinking about the young man grasping the front handle of Jake's casket as I sat next to Sharon in church. "How much were the policies?"

"A million dollars each."

CHAPTER TWELVE

Keeping the Stillman spigot flowing and cashing in on a million-dollar life insurance policy looks like a motive to me. Who needs Jake around when Brian could use the hungry Vo-Tech kids to work on the Mustangs and get that million dollars?

The cold rain soaks me to the bone as I arrive home. At the school, the kids will be settling down for nap time about now. Instead of being there, I'm having visions of autopsy photos, lab results, angry police officers, and gunshot wounds.

I squish into my house and hear hammering upstairs. Ken must be home. The steady downpour probably shortened his workday. I drip water to the laundry room, where I strip off my soaking wet clothes. I scamper to the bathroom and suds up with a warm shower.

We are going to visit my father and stepmother tonight at the retirement village for dinner. It is a standing invitation for all-you-can-eat chicken wings. On the first Wednesday of the month, the village opens its doors to outsiders, with proceeds going to their capital campaign to build a new wing (hence the name of the monthly dinner, "Wings For The Wing"). Many retirement communities have seen a need to offer a special wing for their memory-impaired residents.

After blow-drying my hair, my short Afro returns. I no longer look or feel like a drowned rat. A nice floral dress, sensible flats, and Ken's favorite necklace complete the makeover.

I peek at the faded black-and-white photo kept hidden in my jewelry box. In the photo, I am sitting between my father and my biological mother. I am in my Sunday best, wearing a white dress and matching shoes. My smile is genuine and reminds me I have smiled all my life. People guess me to be ten or fifteen years younger than my fifty-seven. No worry wrinkles stare back at me from the mirror.

In the photo, my father, Stan Wallin, is wearing a dark suit with a white shirt and skinny back tie. I can't decide what his expression is. Being military at the time, you might say he has a military bearing. The photo was taken in England in 1969, when I was almost five, and you might say he borrowed some of the Brit's 'keep calm and carry on' facial expressions for the picture.

Eleanor (it's been nearly a half-century since I called her mom or mother) clutches her purse on her lap. A Jamaican studying nursing in London on a scholarship, she met my father in the infirmary on a Royal Air Force base where he was stationed as she was finishing up her credits. In the photo, she wears a church hat and a dark dress that reminds me of where I get my curves. I do the math and figure I am over thirty years older than she was at the time the picture was taken. Her dark skin is flawless in this shot, but her hands give away her stress. Her expression is one of profound sadness. I don't recall her ever smiling. There may be photos of her in my dad's footlocker where she appears happy, but I don't remember seeing any. Someday, we may have that conversation about what made her perpetually sad. It would be the first since she walked out of our lives the day before I turned six years old. How does a child that young make sense of the yelling, the tears, the hugs, and the ensuing abandonment? Someday, I might get that answer, but today I tuck the photo away with those feelings and remind myself to be grateful for all that I have. I'll have dinner tonight with the parents who loved and raised me, then Sunday dinner with my kids and grandchildren.

I bring my notebook down the hall into my makeshift office. I research the words I didn't understand from both the autopsy and toxicology reports. I add notes to my timeline and stretch red strings on the board between Jake, Brian, and the Stillman twins.

I call Erin a few minutes after four. She allows my adorable grandchildren, Caleb, Jesse, and April, screen time from then until ten minutes before she plates dinner. I fill her in while she readies dinner in the kitchen.

"Mom, Brian told Sharon that Jake died at midnight. Candace tells you he's in cahoots with a couple of lowlifes laundering money and that he stands to collect a million dollars on a life insurance policy he took out on his business partner. Am I missing anything here?"

"Then why would Brian wait until the night before Jake was to marry Sharon to kill him?" I ask her.

"That part stumps me too, she answers. She then shouts away from the phone. "April, put down Chuckles, please. The cat doesn't want to play teatime with you."

Chuckles is a white long-hair rescue kitty they picked up from the pound a few years ago. The cat and April are inseparable, except for times like this.

"I'll have to talk to the other groomsmen, Jake's brothers, about what happened at the cabin before they went home that night," I tell her.

"Anything at the rehearsal dinner of note?" she asks.

"Mabel and Candace said that everybody seemed to have a good time. Both agreed that Becky Steele had a couple too many drinks."

"Do I know her?"

"She was in the same kindergarten class as Sharon and Jake. She was Sharon's maid of honor."

"Can't place her," Erin says.

"She's Reverend Steele's daughter."

"Oh, that's where I know her from. I went to that church a few times for weddings and such."

"That brings up a question I have for you, honey."

"What's that?"

"What was it like for Wes and you going to the school where I was a schoolteacher?"

"I liked it," she says. "We got to see each other every day at school. I enjoyed helping you out on special school projects. If I wasn't feeling well, the nurse would let me go to your classroom to rest."

"Do you think that may have been a factor in you deciding to homeschool Caleb and Jesse?"

"Without a doubt," she says immediately. "I wouldn't have it any other way. When they get to middle school, they will all be in advanced classes, and I get to watch them grow up."

"Did you feel you were swimming in a fishbowl with everybody looking at you because I was a schoolteacher in town?"

She starts laughing. "What?" I ask.

"I'm gonna get all Zen on you, mom. Does the fish know it's in a fishbowl or is that just what normal feels like?"

"So you're saying you didn't know any different. What about Wes?"

"You'll have to ask him."

"Dad said the same thing. He thinks that Wes going through school behind the force of nature known as Erin Strong was intimidating."

"Force of nature? Did he say that?"

"Those were my words, not his."

"Like I said, you'll have to ask him," she says.

"There was a point to me asking you that, because both Mabel and Candace pointed out that the reverend's daughter had too much to drink at the rehearsal dinner. You knew her not from school but from the church. Yvette Strohmeyer, who was also in the same grade, said that Becky grew up in a fishbowl because her dad was a preacher. Her behavior was always being watched and judged."

"Other than Becky Steele having too much to drink, anything about how Jake and his best man were getting along?"

"I may have to go back to Mabel, but Candace didn't get the sense that Brian was going to kill Jake in a couple hours, if that's what you're asking."

"Is it safe to say that maybe what was said or done at the cabin caused Jake's death?" Erin opines.

"So, the gunshot residue on Jake's hand and stippling surrounding the entry wound doesn't make you think it was a death by suicide?"

"It was his non-dominant hand, Mom. Absent a motive, no, I still don't think he shot himself," she says.

"The cops don't know about any motives, and the detective who won't let us look at the file or 911 calls was being cutesy with me about there being no note."

"How so?"

I go back to my notebook and read to her, *"Let's agree there is no note."*

"Why couldn't he just say there was no note?" she asks.

"Could it be something to do with the Stillman twins?" I ask.

"How did you make that jump, Mom?"

"Brian's helping the twins wash their money. Jake knows or figures out where the cash is coming from. Jake wants nothing to do with them anymore. He is getting married the next day and doesn't want his wife to have a husband with a bad reputation for doing shady deals."

"The cops know something about the Stillman twins' illegal activities. Maybe Jake became a weak link and needed to be eliminated. The cops are happy to keep calling this a death by suicide so as not to alert anybody about their investigation into the Stillman brothers," I tell her.

"Until Gwen Strong and her daughter poke around, and they have to pretend to open the case to keep us from getting more information that points towards the guys with a motive to kill Jake," she says.

CHAPTER THIRTEEN

"Your ankles will get stronger the more you practice," Abe says.

I topple over a few times in tree pose and come close to tipping the other yogis over like bowling pins.

"Don't bring your foot to your thigh like the others. Start here," he says as he snugs my left heel against the inside of my right ankle. "With time and repetition, you will get the hang of it."

The lower placement of my foot on my ankle settles my wobble.

He continues, "For now, keep your hands in prayer position in front of your heart. It's more important to establish your tree roots than to spread your branches."

I can do that, and the others don't have to worry about me, Gwen Strong, the human bowling ball.

We work through the other poses without mishap and finish with my favorite corpse pose. Now I know firsthand why my kindergartners loved nap time firsthand. Abe's soothing voice over the soft music works better than melatonin on me.

"How's your investigation coming along?" Emelina asks after the others have departed.

"Could be better, could be worse. I'm planning several interviews today, but I have to be careful not to trip over the police investigation."

"I thought they ruled it a death by suicide," she says.

"They are still calling it that, but they reopened the investigation to keep a nosy kindergarten teacher from looking at the public records."

Abe joins us as we finish stacking mats, bolsters, and blankets. "It's a small town. Somebody will talk to you."

I think about what he said and have an idea. "You are right, Abe. Somebody will talk to me."

"When I walked in, I saw Jake with his head on the table. The left side of his face was lying on the table, and blood was dripping to the floor. He wasn't moving. I checked for a pulse on both his neck and then on his wrist. There was none," Wendy Gallo tells me.

We are standing in the garage bay of the town's EMT station. She offered to meet me there to look at my photos. She is short and dark-haired and spends time at the gym when not working shifts as an EMT. "I didn't want to move the body after determining he was dead. The room still smelled like gunpowder. He was sitting here with his face towards the window. The gun was on the floor here."

She points to one of my photos and places an X where she saw the gun on the floor. She then initials and dates it for me (Erin's advice).

"What kind of gun was it?" I ask.

"I don't know guns. Don't like them after what I have seen on the job."

I produce images of a revolver and then a pistol on my phone.

She points to the pistol.

"Color?" I ask.

"Black with a wood check grip."

"Shell casing on the ground?"

"Wasn't paying attention to that. A guy was standing there in the living room and said he called it in. A girl was in the bedroom. I didn't see her, only heard her sobbing." Wendy checks her run report. "The guy's name is Brian Yelito. He called it in seven minutes after midnight into Saturday morning, said he came into the cabin and saw Jake sitting like that and not moving. About then, Barney showed up."

"What did he do?"

"I told him that Jake was dead. He told me to back off, then he called the State Police. I called dispatch to call off the ambulance that was en route and told them that there would be no hospital transport. Then I grabbed my gear and walked outside. Beautiful clear night. I looked up at the stars and wondered what was so bad that Jake had to kill himself."

"How did you know it was Jake?"

"Yelito told me, said he worked with Jake at a body shop."

"I see," I say. "Do you know if there was a note?"

"I didn't see one, but I didn't look around and I wasn't the first person there. Those other two were there before me."

"What happened next?"

"Barney ushered the guy and the girl outside and stood in the doorway. Nobody else was going in unless it was a state trooper. No sense me hanging around, so I left."

"The girl?" I ask.

"Didn't get a good look at her, but Barney was talking to them like he knew them."

"Thanks, Wendy. I appreciate you talking to me. Do you remember who the dispatcher was that night?"

She smiled. "My sister, Lucinda." You've got to love small towns. She checks her watch. "She's home now. I can call her."

Wendy wakes up Lucinda and introduces me, then hands me the phone. I taught both not so many years ago.

"Hi, Lucinda," I say.

"Hi, Mrs. Strong."

"It's really sad about Jake, isn't it?" I ask.

"Yeah, he was a few years ahead of us in school. I almost died when I heard it was him. Too many young people dying in town these days."

"His mom and dad are having a hard time with it all, and they asked me for help. Do you remember the call?"

"Like it was yesterday. His friend called it in and said that Jake shot himself and was bleeding. He didn't know the address offhand. Friends and family are like that. They know where to go and how to get there, but don't know the street address. He went looking for a piece of mail. I could hear a girl crying in the background until he came back on the line and gave me the address. I dispatched the EMTs and Milford Police. Wendy was first on the scene and said that Jake was unresponsive. Officer Barney Williams then asked for the State Police to respond, and Wendy called off the ambulance coming from the hospital."

"Could you get me times of the calls?" I ask.

"Sure."

"Anything strike you as unusual about this call?"

"Like what?" she asks.

"Anything to suggest motive?"

"Nope, nobody said anything about Jake leaving a note, if that's what you're asking."

"Anybody saying that he didn't do this to himself?"

There is a pause on the line, and I look at Wendy's eyes widen in surprise. Wendy shakes her head. Lucinda says, "Nothing like that, Mrs. Strong."

"Okay."

"One other thing. About ten minutes before midnight. Mr. Chalmers called in complaining of somebody setting off a firecracker. Said something about the idiot not knowing what time of night it was."

"He's Jake's next-door neighbor, isn't he?" I ask.

"Yeah, it wasn't until Jake's friend called with Jake's address that I made the connection."

"Did you mention this coincidence to anybody?" I try to sound nonchalant.

"No, Mrs. Strong. Not until now. Mr. Chalmers calls for any old thing, you know. He's what we call one of our regulars."

"Can you get me that time, too?"

"Sure, Mrs. Strong. Glad to help."

"They had something going on over there that night," Mr. Chalmers tells me. He is a contemporary of Emelina, must be going on ninety. Tall, rail-thin with a halting gait, he uses his cane to point at his neighbor's house through the trees. The front door has yellow and black crime scene tape crossing it. Might as well post a sign—STAY OUT, MRS. STRONG!

We are standing on his porch about fifty yards away. He's old school and would feel uncomfortable with being alone with a woman in his house, so I don't ask to come in. There is a slight nip in the air this morning. Fall will come later this month, but we do get some brisk mornings in September. Still, I rarely have to worry about covering my garden until Columbus Day.

"I was watching a Rambo movie, and with all the commercials, I got up to pee often enough to look out my window. Things got quiet and most of the cars were gone. I know his truck." He pointed to the older white Ford F-150. Ken prefers Fords over

Chevys, especially the model we are looking at. "I'd seen this movie a million times and know the ending, but I stayed up to finish it and was in the bathroom when I heard the shot. It was the last commercial before the big explosions at the end."

I cock my head to ask a question, and he picks up on my move. "I called the cops to tell them somebody was shooting off fireworks. Later, when I saw all the police cars and found out what happened, I figured I heard a shot instead."

"Why'd you think it was fireworks?"

"Didn't think anybody would be shooting a gun at that hour. Besides, it didn't sound like a gun, it was more like a pop. Kids are always whooping it up and carrying on in the woods. I call every time something's not right."

I nod.

He continues. "When you live next to state game land, you know the sound of gunfire. Lived here for close to twenty-five years. Moved here for the peace and quiet, but when small game season starts, it's like a shooting gallery out there." He points to the woodlands leading up to the mountain. "The first day of deer season—forget about it. You hear the shots echoing from dawn to dusk." He shakes his head.

"Anything unusual that night?" I ask.

Mr. Chalmers tells me, "He was having a party. He had no parties, just has his girlfriend over from time to time. Didn't know until later that the boy was getting married the next day. What a shame."

"Does any of this make sense to you, Mr. Chalmers?"

"No, it doesn't." He shakes his head again. "Kids nowadays do the damnedest things."

I didn't think that Sharon would mind sitting in her car while I talked to Mr. Chalmers, and I knew that it would be awkward talking to him with Jake's fiancée staring at him. I fill her in on the way to the county highway department. We have an appointment with Jake's brothers, Dan and Warren Jr., in the yard. I have a question for her though, and I have to be careful how I approach it.

"Becky was to be your maid of honor. When did you guys get close?" I ask.

"When we were growing up. I was friends with lots of girls. As time went by, I was closer with some more than others. Besides school, Becky and I were in youth group at her dad's church throughout high school. When our friends went away to college and moved away after graduation, we were the only ones left."

"How did she react when you asked her to be your maid of honor?"

"She was surprised but said she would do it."

"Sharon, how was she at the rehearsal dinner?"

"She was making eyes at Brian and was getting her courage to chat him up from the free booze. She was playing up the best man-maid of honor thing. He went to Vo-Tech with Jake when we went to the regional high school. Then he and Jake started their body shop. I guess she liked how he grew up."

I sit quietly, thinking about how I want to phrase my next question. "You were all alone at the viewing and would have been all alone at the funeral and cemetery." Sometimes a statement will prompt an answer.

"My parents are still upset they are out of all that money for the wedding. They blame Jake for it. Jake's sisters and brothers circled the wagons around Mabel and Warren."

"Becky?"

Sharon shrugs as she pulls into the parking lot. "Becky's all about Becky. She's a little self-absorbed. The planets and stars revolve around her. I wasn't expecting any comfort from her, if that's what you're asking."

I don't feel the need to tell her about Becky's meltdown at the Dawson home after the interment. Becky had temper tantrums in my classroom. I had more than a few parent-teacher conferences with her folks. In the end, I realized that the man of the cloth couldn't reconcile that his parenting skills might have something to do with her acting out.

Sharon also doesn't have to hear from me that her maid of honor believed that Jake would rather blow his brains out than marry her.

CHAPTER FOURTEEN

The Dawson brothers tell me about the party. Beer and pizza for a couple of hours. Nobody getting out of hand, just them, Jake, and Brian—until Becky showed up with a bottle of Jägermeister. She had gone home and changed into a vee-necked T-shirt, short shorts, and sandals. She was on the prowl for Brian. They were embarrassed to say it to their favorite kindergarten teacher, but Danny finally tells me she was pouring shots into everyone's red cups. When she bent over the table, they couldn't miss the fact that she wasn't wearing a bra. Jake made it clear that he didn't want any part of the booze and he put his hand over the top of his cup, and she poured about an ounce onto his hand. The brothers, being older and wiser, knew that the sooner they made an excuse to leave, the sooner Brian and Becky could hook up. They left her hanging on to him while Jake started cleaning up. They wanted to leave before midnight, and Becky's arrival hastened that decision.

"She uses booze to act slutty," Sharon says of the woman who was supposed to stand next to her at the wedding and say nice things about the bride and the groom at the reception. "She puts on this facade of 'miss goody-two-shoes' around town. To let her freak flag fly, she needs to get plastered. Saw it with her in high school and summers when we were home from college."

"The booze made me do it," I say as we head back into town.

"Exactly."

I reminisce. "I witnessed it firsthand in college. My roommate got drunk and gave herself permission to act stupid. More than a few times, I came back to my dorm room to find a sock on the door and had to sleep in the TV lounge."

"Ouch," Sharon says.

"She's now a big-time lawyer at the state capitol," I say.

"No kidding." Sharon laughs and then asks, "Do you want me to drop you somewhere, Mrs. Strong?"

"Is it going to feel weird calling me Gwen?"

"Yeah, Mrs. Strong. It would be like me calling my mom or dad by their first names."

"No problem, Sharon, I get it. Don't feel that you have to be formal with me, though."

"Okay."

"Let me off here. I need some time to think."

"Going to see Brian at the body shop?"

"An old homicide detective once told me, 'Ain't nothing to it but to do it.' Things happened fast today, and I don't want to just stumble into it." I go through the facts in my mind. Brian and Becky at the after-party. Also, Brian being the 911 caller, not to mention how he kept taking the Stillman twins' cash. I must be careful how I approach the interview.

"Don't forget he was Jake's best friend," Sharon reminds me.

"You're right, honey. That must be my first concern. I am sure that he is hurting." Maybe she'll find out that Brian is about to get a million-dollar payout or that he was laundering money for the Stillman twins, but today is not the day, and I will not be the one to tell her. Not yet.

She lets me out of her car, and instead of walking to the body shop, I take the alley to Yvette Strohmeyer's house a few blocks away from the main drag through town. She and her husband Michael were classmates with Brian, Jake, Sharon, and Becky. Mike, a sheriff, may know something about the Stillman twins.

I approach their small wood shake house, painted gray, from the alley and intercept Mike coming to his truck. He is in gym clothes, toting a lunch box and carrying his uniform on a wooden hanger. He's probably heading off to work out before going in for the evening shift at the jail. Shaved head, short trim goatee, and reflecting sunglasses give off the take-no-crap attitude that goes with his ripped physique. The change in demeanor is apparent when he spots me. "Hi, Mrs. Strong. How are you?"

"I am fine, Michael. How's Yvette?"

"Doc says she's doing fine, but we are getting antsy. Her due date was almost two weeks ago."

"Any talk of inducing her?" I ask.

"No, the doctor says she doesn't want to do that yet with this being our first." He laughs. "We even tried your pepperoni pizza trick, and that didn't work." He reaches for the door handle.

"It was worth the try," I say as he hoists himself into the cab. "I need a minute with you if I can."

He turns the key, and the engine fires up. I walk up to the window as his diesel idles. "Mabel and Warren Dawson have asked me to look into Jake's death."

"Really? I thought that was ruled a death by suicide."

"It was, but nobody can come up with a motive. Barney and the State Police aren't saying for sure there was no note, so the family is scratching their heads."

With the diesel rumbling away, his voice doesn't carry past my ears. "Word is that he didn't want to get married to Sharon."

"I heard that rumor floating around, too."

"Did anybody tell you Jake had a girl on the side?"

"Who?" I try to keep my voice calm and my reaction minimal, but I am reminded why I don't play poker.

"Yvette didn't believe it either when I told her. She thought that Jake and Sharon were soulmates. That's why he and the girl had to sneak around. Barney might know more. He caught them parked down by the river."

I think back to the time before Ken and I were married when things got hot and heavy. I'd be mortified if a police officer had poked his flashlight into the truck at the wrong moment. "Still, is that a reason to shoot yourself in the head?"

"Depends. Could he handle somebody standing up at the wedding and objecting?"

I will admit, I've watched a handful of cringeworthy wedding videos on YouTube with morbid curiosity. "I can see it now that you mention it. Milford's childhood sweethearts. Sharon totally oblivious to Jake's philandering, standing on the altar and getting blindsided. But looking at how's she's suffering now, I think this is a ton worse."

Mike doesn't flinch. "Who said that suicide is a noble act? Maybe Jake couldn't deal with getting outed, and he didn't have the guts to fess up to Sharon."

I do the math. Gunshot residue on his hand. Contact wound to his head. Girlfriend on the side. Happens the night before he is to get married. It all weighs down one side of the scale. Brian and Jake arguing about the Stillman cash and the million-dollar policy rest on the other side of the scale. Pile on the twin's fear that Jake will snitch about their real business, and I have a real tottering scale going on.

I move ahead with my real business for wanting to talk to Mike. "Candace Dawson tells me that Jake and Brian's biggest customers were the Stillman brothers and that they always dealt in cash. Jake and Brian had disagreements about not reporting that income." I shy away from any reference to the cash being dirty or how the Stillmans generate all that cash.

Mike shuts off the truck and stares out the window at me. I have struck a nerve. He shrugs his shoulders. "Not reporting cash to the IRS, so what? I wish I had a nickel for every businessperson who 'forgot' to report cash."

"What if Jake's death was not a death by suicide, Michael? What if it had to do with where the Stillman cash was coming from? You said nothing about them. If somebody killed Jake, why the night before he was to get married?"

For a nanosecond, I see his true reaction before he laughs and says, "I'm sorry, Mrs. Strong, I think you've been watching too many reruns of *Murder, She Wrote.*"

"I don't think I ever watched one, but tell me, Michael, why are you avoiding telling me what you know about the Stillman twins?" I might look up at a buff man in his truck, but to him, his kindergarten teacher is looking down at a six-year-old boy, and she is repeating a question.

At that moment Yvette walks up to us. "Hi, Mrs. Strong." Turning to Mike, she adds, "Is everything okay, honey? I heard your truck stop running."

He smiles at his very pregnant bride and says, "Turned it off to talk to Mrs. Strong for a sec. Told her the pepperoni pizza trick didn't work." He clearly doesn't want to talk in front of her about Jake's murder or the Stillman twins.

"How are you doing, Yvette?" I ask.

"No change. Doc says any day now. Can't wait. I think our baby will be a soccer player though, Mrs. Strong." She holds her bulging belly and groans.

I laugh. "Everything will work out fine, guys." I give her a peck on the cheek. "I will see you later."

I walk in the direction that Mike's truck is facing. I hear him fire it back up again. I wait at the intersection of the alley and the cross street on the sidewalk out of sight for him while he finishes talking with Yvette.

Finally, he pulls up, looking sour. He says, "Mrs. Strong, the Stillman twins are bad news. Jake killed himself because he didn't want to face the music at his wedding. Let it go." He checks both ways again and lurches away from me, leaving me in a black cloud of diesel exhaust.

CHAPTER FIFTEEN

Brian is under the rear of a vintage candy apple red Mustang trying to wrestle a gas tank into place. He is by himself. It's a weekday at this shop, and the Vo-Tech kids don't come in until the weekend. As he taps on something, a cascade of rusty metal flakes blankets his torso. He coughs as he pushes the mechanic's creeper out into my sneakers. He isn't expecting a sudden stop and peels off his dust-covered safety-glasses to stare up at me with a startled expression. "Mrs. Strong, what are you doing here?"

"Looks like you have quite the project, Brian."

"They gave me the wrong size gas tank. It's too big for the brackets." He uses a rag to wipe off his face and neck. "How can I help you?"

"I came to see how you were doing."

He shimmies the creeper away from my feet and sits up. He reaches for a bottle of Mountain Dew and drinks to clear his throat. I worry about how much dust and dirt he must swallow each day, working without a mask. His cough confirms my fears. "I miss the hell out of Jake, and I am angry at him too, leaving all this unfinished work." He waves to the car with the mashed-in nose in the other bay. There are several others like it out on the lot as well. "Then I think about how much pain he must have been in to do that to himself, and I get pissed at myself for being angry with him. Just when I want to feel sorry for little old me, I think about Sharon and the Dawson family."

"It must be awful, Brian. I'm sorry."

He drains the bottle of Mountain Dew, then tosses it towards an open fifty-five-gallon drum, where it bounces off the rim and hits the floor. "He was my best friend and my business partner. More than that, he was the energy behind what we did here. Without him..." He stares at me and then away as moisture creeps into his eyes.

"How long were you best friends?" I ask.

"Since second or third grade."

"Long time. I've spent some time with Sharon since he died and never asked her when they first became boyfriend and girlfriend."

"Had to be fifth or sixth grade. She's the first girl he ever kissed. They went to all the school dances and both proms together."

"Why did he do it, Brian? Mabel and Warren asked me to figure out what had happened. They are just lost."

"I don't know. I keep asking myself that question myself." He slowly gets up and stretches. "He was excited about the wedding. He drank only a little at the rehearsal dinner, and he wanted to get a good night's sleep."

"The Dawson brothers said you guys got a pizza and beer."

"Sure. We went back to his place for a couple of slices and a beer or two." He looked away.

"What?" I ask.

"Becky Steele, Sharon's maid of honor, showed up with a bottle of booze and wanted to party some more. She had too much to drink at the rehearsal dinner. Jake's brothers decided to leave after they had one drink with her."

"What time was that?"

"Before midnight. That's when Jake had decided the party would end."

"How was he then?"

"Little upset with Becky. She was hitting on me at the dinner and then she came over to the cabin and made an ass of herself."

"The reverend's daughter?" I know that question will get a rise out of him.

He reaches for a cigarette and lights it. He blows out smoke and coughs again. "Yeah, that's what everyone thinks." He spits into the trash can. "She came over wearing shorts and a T-shirt. Then she got sloppy with the booze." He looks away from me. "She was too drunk to drive. I decided to take her home. Jake started cleaning up."

"What time was that?"

"Had to be only about ten minutes after his brothers left."

He takes another drag on his cigarette, coughs again, and stares at his steel-toed work shoes. "I got her almost all the way to her parent's house, and she freaks out, telling me she left her bag and purse at the cabin. We drove all the way back and walked in to find Jake at the table. I called 911 and waited."

"What did you and Becky talk about while you waited?"

"Nothing. She completely lost it. Girl was making no sense."

I resist the urge to ask another question. There's more coming.

"Believe me, Mrs. Strong, she's no angel."

"Then what happened?"

"He wasn't moving. I told Wendy I thought he was dead. She checked for a pulse and told Lucinda to cancel the ambulance."

"What about Becky?"

"She sat in Jake's bedroom and just cried her eyes out. Officer Williams came in next and told everybody they had to get out."

"Did anybody look for a note?"

"It was pretty obvious to everyone he shot himself." He looks at me like I somehow missed the obvious.

"I'm sorry, Brian. Did anybody look for a note? The reason I ask is that when I asked Barney and the State Police, they said to me, 'Let's agree there was no note.' Do you understand now why I am asking?"

"I can't tell you if there was a note or not. I just stood there staring at him until Wendy came in."

"Where was Becky?"

"She was puking her brains out and then stayed in Jake's room while Wendy and I waited for Officer Williams."

"What happened next?"

"He came in, asked Wendy if Jake was dead, then called for the State Police. He asked us all to go outside and wait for them. It was a while before they showed up. I told him everything I just told you. He was gonna call Jake's parents, but I told him I would. He didn't know that Jake was getting married the next day. I told him about the rehearsal dinner and the guys having one last drink with Jake as a single guy."

"Did he take any photos?"

"Nope." Jake lights another cigarette from the first. He's in no hurry to wrestle with the gas tank.

I look at the car and already know the answer to the question I ask. "Whose car is that? You don't see many old Mustangs like that anymore."

"A couple of brothers. You don't know them, they didn't go to school with us. They buy 'em wrecked and sell 'em around the country after we fix them up."

"I think Candace mentioned something about them."

"Yeah, Candace would. What a pain in the butt, Mrs. Strong." I cock my head. "They always pay in cash. Jake and I always wanted cash customers if you know what I mean."

"I do. My husband does 'cash favors' for townsfolk occasionally." I wink. I can give a little to get a little.

"Candace convinced Jake that everything had to be run through the books. Jake and I would have our arguments about how to work on the cars, you know, whether to repair or replace some parts, but we left the books up to her. Jake told her he wasn't working on their cars anymore and that I would use their cash to buy their parts, but he didn't tell her he and I still split what they paid us. I got a couple of kids from Vo-Tech to come in on weekends to work as interns. They love working on the classics. The pictures of the restored ponies would go into their portfolios. They could get a job anywhere with proof that they worked on those cars. We figured a way to keep Candace happy. Nothing would show up in the books for those cars, and we'd still keep the cash."

I can see where Jake might tell Candace one thing and do another, especially after hearing how he might have had a side girlfriend. Brian and Jake were best friends. And best friends are not family. I'm sure there are things about Erin or Wesley that I know nothing about, but their best friends certainly have the inside dope.

"Tell me about the life insurance policies that you took out on each other."

"What life insurance policies?" He looks genuinely puzzled. "Mrs. Strong, what are you talking about?"

"Candace said that you both had life insurance policies taken out on each other."

He shakes his head. "I signed a bunch of papers when we started the business. I don't remember them all. Like I said, we let Candace handle the books. She'd tell Jake what we needed to know, and he'd tell me. As long as we were making more money each year, I didn't care about the numbers."

"Brian, you were his beneficiary, and he was yours."

"So what? They probably won't pay off." He crushed out his cigarette on the side of the drum.

"Why do you say that?" I ask.

"Because he killed himself, Mrs. Strong. Isn't that like against the law? Nobody gets anything if you kill yourself."

I can't help but think that Barney and Detective Shafer should be here listening to this. Then again, if they weren't so quick to close the case, they might rule out suspects like I am now. Still, I can't bring myself to tell Brian that the period of contestability for a death by suicide has expired and that he will receive a million dollars. I can turn over that card some other time.

Unless… I look up and stare at this boy. I think about him at church carrying the casket. I remember him and Jake in my class and them playing in the schoolyard. I recall those two riding on their bicycles like maniacs around town. Unless, of course, he would be excluded from collecting if he murdered Jake. "I'm not sure how that works," I lie.

"Can you let me know if you find anything out, Mrs. Strong? I'd like to know why he did this to himself and to us."

"Yes, Brian, I can." I turn to look at the Mustang. It wants to tell me something, but I am not sure what it is. "What are you going to do about that?" I point to the gas tank.

"Tell them to take it back. I can't make it fit, and I'm not going to break my neck trying."

CHAPTER SIXTEEN

"How long do you think Brian and Becky were away from the cabin, Mom?" Erin asks after I tell her about my day.

I look at my timeline on the blackboard in my office as I talk to her on the phone. "Half hour, tops. The Dawson boys left after eleven thirty. Brian says they stayed around for one drink with Becky, then he took her home. Mr. Chalmers says he hears a 'pop' during the last commercial before the end of the movie he's watching. He made the noise complaint about ten minutes before twelve. Then Brian Yelito calls it in seven minutes after midnight."

"Wendy smells the gunpowder when she enters the cabin," Erin reminds me.

"That is what she said," I reply.

"Do we know when she arrived?" she asks.

"Nope, but I can find out easily enough."

"Doors and windows closed would keep the smell inside longer," she says. I can hear the kids arguing about the TV in the background. "Wait a minute, Mom." I hear her banish my precious grandchildren to their rooms with the threat of no electronics for the night if she hears another peep from them. "I'm back."

"I can ask Brian again about the windows," I say.

"What do you think about Brian, Mom?"

"I can circle back with Sharon and Candace about how savvy Brian was in the business," I tell her.

"What do you make about him not naming the Stillman twins to you?" she asks.

"He told me that I didn't know them, which is true, and I didn't think he needed to identify a big cash customer he was hiding from the government to his former kindergarten teacher."

"Agreed," she says.

"Did I tell you he was working on a Stillman Mustang when I showed up?"

"No, Mom, you failed to supply me with that fact."

"He was upset that he had the wrong parts and had to return them. That's how I could bring up them being cash customers without naming them."

"Smooth. What do you think about him now?"

"He has an alibi with Becky Steele. The Dawson brothers left them while Jake was cleaning up, and Wendy saw them when she arrived. If drunk Becky hadn't forgotten her purse, people would show up at the cabin the next day wondering why he wasn't at the church and find his corpse."

"What about the Stillmans?" she asks.

"Would he be seated at a table like that if they came in uninvited after everybody had left him alone?" I ask her back.

"Maybe they pretended to make a deal with him and caught him by surprise," she says.

"I can't disagree with you, Erin."

"You're doing the double negative thing on me again, Mom. Why can't you agree with me?"

"Just need to think it out. I learned a great deal today and I want to process it, that's all," I explain to my sharp as a tack daughter.

Ken walks into my makeshift office and waggles his cell phone at me.

"Hold on, Erin."

Ken says, "Brian Yelito left a voice message saying that he forgot to tell you something important and to call him. He said he didn't know how to reach you, so he tried me."

"Did you hear that, Erin? I am going to call him back before he changes his mind."

"Okay, Mommy. Let me know what happens."

"Will do. Love 'em and hug 'em, honey." I end our call.

Ken asks me, "What's going on?"

I fill him in as I call Brian back. It goes to voicemail. Then I text Brian and get no response. I look at the time. It's not too late, and it's still light out.

"Ken, can we stop over at the body shop and go out for dinner after I talk to Brian? I got too busy with everything to defrost the leftovers."

He tells me about his day on the short trip. Ken parks in the lot and I tell him I will only be a minute. I am wondering what Brian will tell me as I walk into the bay with the Mustang. It is shrouded in late afternoon shadows, and he didn't turn the overhead lights on. I approach him as I did earlier in the day. His legs are splayed out under the side of the car. My eyes adjust to the darkness.

Suddenly, I have no appetite. The left rear axle is trying to touch the garage floor except for the fact that Brian's torso is in the way.

CHAPTER SEVENTEEN

"It was an accident, Mrs. Strong." Detective Shafer walks back to me. "The hydraulic trolley car lift collapsed. That's the preliminary finding. They are going to examine it back at the lab to be sure." I had already told him and Barney Williams the story twice about how I interviewed Brian earlier and came back to the garage after he didn't answer his phone. I noticed something different between my two visits and decided to hold that back from the police until they gave me their version.

We are standing outside of the garage bay, having been there since they taped off the scene. Ken and I shiver together arm in arm as our summer clothes are not warm enough in the darkness. A cool breeze kicks up.

I'm not buying that this was an accident. "Don't you think it's strange, detective, that the owners of this body shop die within a week of each other?"

"You said it yourself, Mrs. Strong. Yelito was mad Dawson killed himself and left him with all this work to do. Maybe he was exhausted and got careless. He should have been using floor mounts to suspend the rear end as a back-up."

"Or maybe it's something else," my daughter pipes up from behind me.

Shafer gives her a puzzled look.

"Detective Shafer, say hello to my daughter, Erin LeGrande." Erin hands Ken and me each a heavy pullover sweater. I didn't even ask her to bring them. Next, she hands us both a couple of large Dunkin' Donut coffees. I love this girl.

He smirks. "The Erin LeGrande whose FOI request caused me to have to reopen the Dawson death?"

"Yes," she says, "and how is that coming along, Detective Shafer?"

"It's an open investigation," he says dryly. "No comment."

"Two deaths in less than a week, best friends under suspicious circumstances," I say.

"Both deaths are unwitnessed. What are the odds of that?" Erin adds.

The detective seems unaccustomed to being questioned by civilians and is not a happy camper. I spot Barney Williams staying clear of us. I have questions for Barney and remind myself to catch him at the right time.

"Maybe I should just let you two amateurs run the show," he says.

"Notice how he didn't answer your question, Erin. Aren't you glad, Detective Shafer, that I called the State Police barracks on a recorded line asking specifically for you, saying that this death is connected to the Dawson case you are working?"

I notice Ken start to drift away, but only to shake his coffee and not spill it on himself. He is still close enough to hear the conversation.

"What's that supposed to mean?" Shafer says as he stares at me. I may have poked the sharply dressed plainclothes law enforcer a little too hard.

"It means that as much as Erin and I would love to figure this out, you were the first person I called." I give him an equally hard stare. "I didn't call for an ambulance or that guy over there." I point to the oversized officer wearing an undersized uniform. "If this turns out to be an accident, so be it, but I made sure that nobody trampled all over your crime scene."

He gulps as he realizes I am right. "Who would want him dead?"

"Who would want *them* dead?" I remind him.

"Okay, who would want them dead?"

I point to the Mustang. "Follow the money. If both deaths are not what they appear, who would have the motive to kill them?" I ask.

Ken had wanted to jack the Mustang up and extricate Brian from underneath, but I knew my former student was dead as soon as I squatted down and looked at his face and saw a gray death mask. His hand was cold to the touch. I pushed my helpful husband away from the jack and I told him it may contain fingerprints or DNA. Brian hadn't answered his phone or checked for text messages because he had already been killed.

Erin and I had talked this out well before Williams, and then Shafer rolled up on the scene. After I called the barracks, I took photos in the fading sunlight of the scene while my daughter calmed me down and told me what to do and say until she could drop the kids off at her in-laws before meeting me here. We were ahead of the cops and had to think like steely-eyed professionals, lest we be treated the way we were when we had started looking into Jake's death.

"Is that a rhetorical question?" Shafer asked, bringing me out of my thoughts.

"Maybe," Erin replied.

"That depends on what you already know, detective," I add. "If neither death is as it appears, then who would want them dead? If you reopened the first case to keep us from stepping into something you are working on, then you already have a pretty good idea on motive."

Erin stands shoulder to shoulder with me and asks, "If you reopened the Dawson death just to thwart our efforts, then you are just finding out tonight that the deaths may be connected. Which is it?"

We get our answer when Shafer says to the crime scene technicians, "We are taking the Mustang too." He walks over to Williams in a huff, and they confer briefly before going off in different directions. It appears the boys in blue have a little catching up to do.

Chinese takeout is a treat in the Strong household. Having one of my children over to the house mid-week is special. Staring at my shell-shocked husband, I am wondering what I got myself and Erin into. I cannot enjoy the shrimp with garlic sauce over brown rice before me. That's not to say that I am not devouring my late-night dinner.

"Whaddya thinking, Mom?" Erin asks me.

"It's more important that we ask how your father is doing," I reply.

Ken stares at us from the head of the table. "I felt like I walked on to a movie set, but it was all too terribly real."

"What else?" I work my chopsticks around the plate. I know I am putting my man on the spot, and I don't want to stare at him.

"Then I watched my wife and daughter acting like a couple of hard-boiled gumshoes."

I see Erin suppress a grin. "Which ones, Daddy?"

He rolls his eyes at her. "I mean it. There is a dead guy on the ground, and you two were talking to the detective like you would to one of your kids."

"I would never talk to my kids like that," she protests.

"It seems surreal to me too, honey," I say. "Things got crazy for me in a big way. What was I thinking?"

He swirls the last of his eggroll into a puddle of duck sauce. "I felt like an innocent bystander to the whole thing and there was nothing I could do for you guys."

"You stood by me and trusted me, even though I was way over my head. That's what you did, Kenneth Strong."

"Okay, why don't you explain it to me then?" he says. "There were a lot of things not spoken between you two and the detective."

"I didn't think Jake's death was as first claimed. Then I found out his business partner, Brian, was dealing with some unsavory characters and stood to gain from a million-dollar life insurance policy. Seeing Brian at the funeral and then talking to him today, though, I didn't think he had anything to do with Jake's death."

"Not directly," Erin pipes in.

"Yes, not directly. When I saw Brian dead on the floor of their garage. I realized that Jake's death was murder and Brian's death was made to look like an accident. That's why I insisted that the detective looking at the one had to look at the other. I was forcing him to make the connection."

"They didn't treat Jake's cabin like a crime scene," Erin adds, "and Mom would not let that happen again."

"What was all that talk about? A rhetorical question?" Ken asks. "That went right over my head."

"Erin and I are troubled. When they stiff-armed us after we made our records request, we questioned whether they had something they were working on and wanted to keep us at arm's length, or maybe they just didn't want to get embarrassed by questions we would raise," I tell him.

"And?"

Erin finishes my thoughts a little more bluntly. "And we find out tonight they had nothing and weren't doing jack-squat."

"We are forcing their hand to do something about both deaths now," I add.

"Are you going to leave it up to them now that you have their attention?" Ken asks.

I look at Erin. She looks at her father, then back at me. "That's a great question, Mommy. Are we going to leave it to Foghorn Leghorn and our good friend Detective Shafer?"

"I don't know."

"You said something about unsavory characters." Ken knows how to push his bride's buttons, too.

"Candace Dawson is the bookkeeper for Jake and Brian. She said they had a regular customer who bought wrecked Mustangs and paid for everything in cash. Everything. She went so far as to find out from the truck dealerships where they bought their brand-new trucks that they paid cash for the down payment and were paying the monthlies with a casino debit card."

"You going to tell me who the unsavory characters are?"

There it was. Dare I say their names out loud to my husband? "Simon and Jason Stillman. They didn't grow up here. They came when they were in high school." I hold my breath.

Ken stiffens. "I know those two smartasses. Acting like bigshots. Think they can push people around acting all tough as they drive their shiny trucks around town."

Both Erin and I look at each other. "And?" we ask at the same time.

"And none of the contractors can figure out what they are up to. They hire out-of-state contractors to come in work for them. Just like you say, they pay cash. Best we can tell, they act like preppers."

"Preppies, like they went to prep school?" Erin asks.

"No, preppers, like those people who think that world is going to collapse any minute and they have to prepare for it. Survivalists."

"Do you know where they live?" I ask.

"Why? Are you thinking of paying them a social call, Gwendolyn?"

I don't get addressed as Gwendolyn very often by my husband. Usually, he has good reason. But sometimes I push his buttons, and I just pushed one. "No, I am curious. What makes you say that?"

"All that living 'off the grid' stuff their contractors order and pay cash for at the contractor's registers. Generators, water filtration parts. Solar grids and converters. Hot house stuff." He pauses. "Guns and ammo, too. You'd think they plan to hold out in the hills against the zombies. Those guys are either crazy or really dangerous."

"Or both." Erin says. I have a feeling it's going to be a late night for her tapping away on the computer.

"Then why are they restoring Mustangs?" I ask. "You'd think they'd be working on old off-road vehicles with mechanical ignitions and starters."

Both my husband and daughter look at me strangely.

"So, when the atmospheric electromagnetic pulse bomb knocks out all the computers, they can still drive around."

Their looks don't change.

"You think all I read on my Kindle are steamy romance novels?" I ask.

"Do you think the cops know about these guys?" Erin asks. I see her mind churning on this. She might ask for a favor from her part-time employer.

Ken shrugs. "Nothing illegal, I can tell. They act like they got a ton of money, and they flash it around."

I know my daughter, and she is getting antsy to get home and research the Stillman twins. I take the cue. "Well, it's late, and somebody has to get up in the morning and teach."

"Let me know what you decide," she says.

"I'll walk you out, honey. I won't be long, Ken. I'm exhausted."

Once outside, she says, "I'll let you know what I find on them." She hugs me tightly. Our investigation is less than a week old, and it has gotten a lot scarier.

"One other thing I didn't mention to Shafer or your father," I say. I glance back at the house to be sure my beloved is out of earshot. "I noticed the gas tank that Brian wanted to return was nowhere to be found."

CHAPTER EIGHTEEN

Ken and I toss and turn all night. Daylight cannot come early enough. Robotically, we go about our morning hygiene until it's time to meet at the kitchen table. He tells me, as he fills his thermos, that he's going to bounce around to check on several quotes and talk to people that are on the fence about getting some work done before winter. He'd then finish some trim work upstairs. His major rehab client probably got a text that Ken wouldn't be tearing things up today. I understand why for two reasons. First, he doesn't want to be around heavy-duty power tools when he's exhausted. Second, he learned a craftworker died by either carelessness or at the hands of a killer. I imagine it's hard to concentrate on skilled labor today either way.

My mind had spent all night in overdrive, churning the clues and recalling my conversation with the State Police detective. I know also that my daughter will give me an update on the Stillman twins. A decision will have to be made. I see myself staring at Mabel and Sharon at different times today, telling them about Brian's death. Both Brian and Jake's families will receive the life insurance benefits. That won't bring their boys back, but a million bucks with help them salvage something from this terrible week. I will go to Brian's memorial service. Knowing that I may have been the last person he talked to weighs heavily on my mind. To think that twenty-four earlier, he was my number-one suspect in the murder of his best friend. Seeing his dead eyes staring at me made me question why I was even thinking that I could investigate a suspicious death. How do I offer my condolences to his family? *Gee, Mr. and Mrs. Yelito, I am sorry for your loss, but at least I eliminated your darling son as a murder suspect.* At some point, I will talk to Becky Steele and close out that last lead, if only for my curiosity.

Then there is the thought that my curiosity, my grandiose thinking that I could solve Jake's murder, may have led to Brian's death. Somebody had to get to him before he told me something incriminating about them. That thought bounces around my head for hours as I try to dispassionately review all the facts. Did Jake's killer know that I was foraging for clues and that killing Brian would stop my progress?

"You look like crap," Ken says to me.

I don't take the truth as an insult. "I feel like crap."

"What's your plan for the day?"

"I'm waiting to hear from Erin. She will give me a quality intelligence briefing on the Stillman twins. If there is something there, I will turn everything over to Detective Shafer, and if he's not responsive, then I'll take it to his boss. I won't let him push us aside."

"You let him know last night that you are no pushover. I don't know what bothered me more, finding the dead kid or watching you play hardball with a guy who just happens to carry a badge and a gun around here."

I push back gently, "C'mon Ken, you've seen me get that way in school when I knew something wasn't right."

"Yeah, but school principals and administrators are just bigger goldfish in the fishbowl. You were swimming in a shark tank last night."

"Or maybe I've been swimming with sharks since I decided to look into Jake's death." My toast pops and I slather jam on it. Sugar always helps, and this morning I can use the dopamine hit.

"Meaning?" he asks.

"In the wee hours of the morning, while we were both twisting and turning, I had the thought that by sticking my nose where it didn't belong, I may have caused Brian's death."

"How?"

"Everybody was satisfied with the obvious. Jake shot himself. The cops don't care why. The cops were satisfied that the evidence pointed that way. The only person to offer a motive is the bride's maid of honor, who said Jake put a bullet in his head rather than marry his childhood sweetheart the next day." I take a breath, then continue. "I saw the insurance policy and the argument over the Stillman twins as Brian's motive for killing Jake. By not accepting his death's official ruling, I kept the ball in play. I made a nuisance of myself with the Milford Police and the State Police. Word got around that Jake's kindergarten teacher, who has nothing better to do, is asking questions. What does Brian know that got him killed? What did I do to get him killed?"

I can't hold my feelings in any longer. The tension from the previous evening. The sleepless night. Ken being a witness to something terrible that he will never forget. It all causes me to release a flood of sobbing tears.

He comes around to my side of the table and lets me cry into his shoulder. He holds me gently and doesn't let go until my phone buzzes on the table. We both look to see a picture of Chuckles the cat on my screen.

"It's Erin, I gotta take it." I walk upstairs as I answer and open my composition notebook. I had put nothing in there about last night. I may never.

"Hi, Mom," Erin says. "How are you doing?"

"Well, I just told your father that I got Brian Yelito killed."

"That must have been some breakfast conversation," she says.

"What did you get on the Stillman twins?" I ask as I stare out the window. I tap a blank page in the notebook absent-mindedly.

"They are into that prepper stuff big time. Simon is the big talker on social media. He is an influencer in their movement. They travel around country, and they are sought-after expo speakers. It looks like they are resellers of high-end stuff that the preppers buy like crazy, and they also do affiliate marketing from their websites. You know those corrugated shipping containers you see the big rigs pulling on the interstate?"

"Yeah," I say, wondering where this is going.

"These guys will ship you one that is completely tricked out to survive World War III. It's their brand, and they own the market. All the gadgets are American made, and they do the assembly in Mobile, Alabama from discarded containers they buy as salvage. They get the prospects to talk to sales professionals who close the deals on a pure commission basis, who then hand off the contract to their fulfillment center. They act and talk like good ole boys, but they are grossing a couple mil a year. I'll send you the link to the last expo where they showcased their containers."

"What do your friends say about them?" Erin has friends in high places—like FBI headquarters.

"I sent the intel along and made a query. Said it was to do with a couple suspicious deaths of the owners of a body shop where they were having a Mustang rebuilt."

"What about the cars?"

"That's what I had to wait on 'til this morning. Besides their trucks and a couple travel trailers and old-school Harleys, they don't show any Mustangs bought or sold in the last five years."

"How can that be?" I ask. I toy with the string on the corkboard connecting Brian and Jake to the Stillmans.

"Open titles, Mom. They buy the cars and never put their name on the title as the buyer because they never register them. That is the answer I got. If the body shop recorded any of the VIN numbers, you'd see that the Stillmans bought the wrecks and shipped the cars to the buyers with the open title for their buyers to fill in their names on the title. You won't see Simon or Jason's names on the titles."

"What does that tell you, Erin?"

"The cars can never be traced to the Stillmans. Jake and Brian were the only links to them."

"And now they are dead." I sob again as I close my notebook and drag down the strings from the board.

She waits for me to stop. She's a good daughter.

"I can't disagree with you, Mom," she says. Two can play my game of using double negatives.

"Why's that, honey?"

"We knocked over a hornet's nest. What do you want to do about it?"

"Can you get the motor vehicle records showing that the Stillmans didn't own any Mustangs?"

"Why?"

"I want us to bring everything to Shafer, and if he won't listen to us, to Shafer's boss, so we can lay all our cards on the table."

"Including the missing gas tank?"

"Including the missing gas tank," I say.

"Why?" she asks

"Why? Maybe because you are a stay-at-home mom that home-schools her adorable children, and I am a recently retired kindergarten teacher who looked into the blank stare of a murder victim yesterday. We are not homicide investigators. I never thought I'd be looking at dead bodies in the flesh." I say it to myself as much as to Erin. It finally hits home. I witnessed by first murder victim in the flesh yesterday.

Erin is telling me about the rest of her Stillman research as I walk downstairs. Ken has left for the day. I will catch up with him around lunchtime and tell him my decision.

I step outside into the misty drizzle of a gray morning. There are a few cucumbers and peppers ready to be picked in my garden. I reach for my basket, then interrupt Erin. "I'm sorry, honey, but I think we found the motive for both Jake and Brian's deaths. They figured out whatever the Stillmans were up to, and they died because of it. I can tell Mabel and Sharon something after we talk to Shafer. We forced him to reopen an apparent death by suicide and a supposed accident as homicides and we are pointing him at the logical suspects. Our work is done here, Honey." I ring off without telling her to love and hug my adorable grandchildren.

CHAPTER NINETEEN

"We've talked about this before, Gwen," my father says.
"I have no memory of her ever smiling. Do you have any photos of her smiling, Dad?" I show him the photo I pinched from his footlocker all those years ago of me sitting between him and my birth mother when I was five years old. "Was she ever happy?"

I took the retirement community shuttle to his place this morning. I just needed to get out of Dodge and think about something other than dead bodies.

We are sitting in the living room of his comfortable apartment. The TV is muted, a silenced distraction hanging on the wall across from us. Our knees are almost touching as we sit facing each other at an angle on his love seat. He is much taller and thinner than me. His hair is silver, and unlike most former military men, he has let it grow over his ears to touch his collar. My stepmom is bringing a sick friend and her husband some soup and sandwiches for lunch. It gives Dad and me time to talk about something she doesn't have to feel obligated to listen to for the umpteenth time.

"We only knew each other for a short time before she learned that she was pregnant," he says. This is the first time he tells me about their courtship, and I am surprised by it.

"Are you saying that you didn't love each other?"

"She took a liking to me, and I took a liking to her." He touches her face in the photo. "You can see where you got your good looks from." He sets the photo on the coffee table. "We both were in a place where we knew that we'd both be moving on. We just gravitated towards each other. Some things happened faster than others." He shrugs. "I offered to marry her, and she accepted. She wasn't looking for an American husband while finishing up her nursing degree at an infirmary on a Royal Air Force base in England. She planned to return to Jamaica to become a nurse and resume her life there."

"I knew it. I knew I was a mistake." I had never said those words out loud to him before.

"No, honey. You were and are Stan Wallin's lovely daughter. I loved you from the minute they let me hold you."

"But Eleanor didn't." I step over a line.

"How old are you now?" he asks me.

"I'm fifty-seven, you know that," I gently scold him.

"You are old enough to know now that your mother probably suffered from postpartum depression. She may have been clinically depressed on top of that. None of us knew what that was back then, that it was a real thing." He stops to sip his coffee.

I have never considered that possibility. What did I know about depression?

He continues. "Jean and I have lots of friends here at the village, and we are learning about all kinds of illnesses. People here are very vocal about who has what. No sense hiding anything at this stage of the game. Depression runs right behind high-blood pressure, diabetes, and the big C for ailments around here."

I am understanding how my father would see his new friends

behave and then look back at those similar signs of depression in my mom.

"Consider this for a minute," he goes on. "On top of an undiagnosed chemical imbalance, she was all alone. When I had to travel for work, I left a mind-sick young mother with a colicky baby. She had no family there. She was one of only a few black people on the base or in the town nearby. Let me remind you that this was the 1960's, Gwen. England was a little better than America in race relations." He held his thumb and index finger an inch apart. "But just a little. I know. I was married to a Black woman."

He takes a deep breath and stares into my eyes. "It's high time I ask you to stop acting like an abandoned six-year-old and put yourself in her shoes. Why don't you take a few minutes and do just that? I'm right here, and I am not going anywhere."

I start to say something but look down instead. The way he said it was not a reprimand, but a heartfelt request.

I reach out for his right hand with my left, and we sit closer while I close my eyes and breathe deeply, slowly in and out. I have never looked at the situation from her point of view before. I imagine myself to be my birth mother. Every time my own anger or resentment wells up from those familiar places in my heart, I gently release those feelings and return to putting myself in her place.

Alone and Black in a lily-white world, Jim Crow talks with a clipped British accent. Pregnant by a man I barely know. Scared and maybe ashamed. No, there is no maybe. I am ashamed. Away from home and everyone I know. I've given birth in a sterile-white British hospital, then was sent home. I'm abandoned for long stretches of time with a crying baby.

When these thoughts start to fade, I return to my steady and deep, rhythmic breathing.

I imagine life in the English countryside. It's nothing like

Kingston. In my mind, I see and taste the bland food. I listen to their white pop music on the radio.

I am slightly aware of my body, but in my mind, I am there in England.

Nothing is as I planned. I stare at this infant in my arms as it cries and cries. My newlywed husband is at work, and I can't reach him.

My breath now catches. I feel the anxiousness well up, that chest-tightening, star-seeing, pulsing red-light before my eyes panic.

I force myself to keep my eyes closed, and I am there in that desperation, that utter loneliness, with a shattered self-worth, a screaming baby in my arms. It is dark. The officers' housing is cold from the winter wind blowing outside. I have never felt this cold before in my life. I shiver.

I see the baby as a toddler now. The little girl wants to play, and her father allows her to ride on his back until his knees are raw from the threadbare carpet. I see the happiness on their faces. Slowly, the panic attack subsides. I return to deep breathing in and out. I don't need to count. Slowly in and slower out after a pause.

I see the young girl in the photo is going to the American school on base. She can be cared for now. She's a happy kid and her father loves her. They will be all right.

As I breathe in and out, tears fill my eyes, and I begin to sob. My sobbing becomes louder and my breathing more difficult. The waves of feelings well up from deep within me, a place in my heart long guarded by the childhood scars, the feeling of being unwanted by my mother.

My father's hand moves up my arm and then around my shoulder. I feel him hold me now as my sobbing increases. A lifetime of anger, resentment, fear of not being good enough melts into his embrace, like the biblical banishing of an unclean spirit.

I open my wet eyes, and my dad scurries to the kitchen and

brings back a wad of paper towels. I blow my nose and wipe my eyes, then reorient myself to place and time.

"Do you want to talk about it, Gwen? You were somewhere else for the last forty-five minutes."

"I walked in Ele—my mother's shoes just like you asked."

"Where'd you go? St. Louis?" He snorts softly. He appears relieved that I returned from the trip.

I laugh. "I've started meditating this week, and I guess your suggestion was all I needed today to go where I've been afraid to go all my adult life."

"And?"

"I never made the leap from how everything affected me to how everything affected her. Adding that she was probably prone to depression made it easier for me to be—to feel—to see her side, and to…" I can't find the word to describe my feeling.

"To cut her some slack," he says.

"More than that." Slowly, the words come. "To feel compassion for her and all the things that she had to have suffered through."

"And?"

"C'mon, Daddy. You're doing to me what I did to my kindergarteners."

"And?" he persists.

"And I turned out okay." The words spill out without a brain filter. Straight from my heart to my mouth. I feel it for the first time. I turned out okay. I am not damaged property.

"No, honey," he says. "You turned out wonderful." It is his turn to have misty eyes.

CHAPTER TWENTY

It's Saturday morning and sunny. Breezy, with the promise of a nice day ahead. Abe has a packed studio for both meditation and yoga. Shavasana is the Sanskrit word for corpse pose. I will always call it shavasana from now on, and I ask Abe to do the same after I relate to him and Emelina the last corpse I saw and how it wasn't posing.

Emelina says, "Gwen, what did you get yourself into?"

"Worse," I reply, "I exposed Ken to the whole mess."

Abe helps us stack the mats, blankets, bolsters, and blocks. His playlist has shifted from woo-woo flutes, bells, and chants to a Tower of Power funky jazz play list. "And you look at this as a failure? I didn't realize Milford was whine country."

Both Emelina and I look at him. He stares back. "C'mon Mrs. Strong, you, as an educator, more than any layperson know what the acronym FAIL stands for."

"Sorry Abe, I must have slept through that class."

He turns to Emelina. "Ms. Bidwell, don't tell me you don't know either?"

"Enlighten us, Oh Great One." She does a deeper bow than I could ever attempt.

"FAIL stands for First Attempt In Learning. What did you fail at, and what can you learn from the experience?" he asks me.

"I wasn't prepared to encounter a dead body, especially of one of my former students."

"You were going to add something else," he says.

"I wasn't expecting my number one suspect to become the next murder victim in a matter that I was investigating." Lately, it has become easier to just speak my truth.

"What if you had gone in there to talk about getting an estimate for your car?"

"I don't have a car, Abe."

He shakes his head. "Hypothetically, then."

"I'd believe that I walked in on an unfortunate accident."

"And what if you didn't know him personally?"

"I'd say that I came upon a tragic event. The memory of his body would fade with time, I imagine," I tell them.

"From what I understand, you also convinced the police to re-investigate the first boy's death and to look more closely into what you saw at the auto body shop."

I nod.

"And you may have uncovered a motive."

"In less than a week's time," Emelina chimes in.

"You were exactly the right person to walk in when you did. Nobody else would have seen what you saw beyond the obvious."

"Well, that is one way of looking at things," I admit.

"What if every police officer, firefighter, and emergency room worker quit after they saw their first dead body in the line of duty?"

I have him now. "But it's not my job—"

He interrupts me with a fiery look. "No, Mrs. Strong. What you embarked upon was way more than a paycheck. You followed your calling. You have found your calling. I am afraid this won't be the first dead body that you will observe. You must persevere."

"If I don't?"

"Then you will regret quitting for the rest of your life. That will be the failure."

"Don't you think that's a little harsh, Abe?" I ask. I am not expecting to be stung by someone I hardly know.

"Does it make it any less true?" He zings me good. Abe's right, dammit. *Gwen Strong, Quitter*. I roll that around on my tongue for a bit, then I look back and forth between them. Emelina was always my mentor, and Abe is becoming my guru.

"This is just your first time at the rodeo, Gwen," Emelina tells me.

"You guys are something else."

"Thank you," they say in unison, and both bow towards me.

I bow back. "Namaste."

I walk out to the sidewalk in the brilliant sunshine. My head is spinning from the lesson I just received, and I am not talking about downward dog. Between my revelation yesterday about my birth mother and this tough love talk from two people who I admire, I am finding it all that I can do to place one foot in front of the other as I make my way to the market.

To say that my world has been turned upside down is an understatement, but I realize that I am walking lighter without a lifetime's baggage, and Abe has helped me gain perspective over Brian's death and what I must do.

Gene Autry's "Back in the Saddle Again" comes to mind, and when I sing along in my head, I am back on the case.

Just then, a vehicle stops ahead of me along the curb next to the sidewalk. I don't pay it much attention, as I'm in my own little song world. The passenger hops down from the truck. It's bright shiny blue with fancy wheels. The young man closes the distance to me. He is dressed right out of an L.L. Bean catalogue. The clean boots tell me he has scaled no mountains lately. He smiles and extends a hand, and I automatically reach to shake it. Office hands, as my husband would derisively call them, soft and manicured.

The man speaks while still holding my hand in a soft but firm grip. "Hello, Mrs. Strong, my name is Simon Stillman. I believe this is the first time we have met."

"Good morning, Mr. Stillman," I say coolly. A gazillion thoughts pulse through my skull in a nanosecond, but none of them are sparking a flight or fight response.

"Simon, please." He releases my hand. Should I be alarmed? I don't feel threatened by him.

"I am on my way to the market," I say.

"May I walk with you? There is something I need to discuss with you, and the fresh air will do me good."

I stay on the right side of the sidewalk, and he catches my stride to my left.

"Your daughter and the State Police have recently taken an interest in my brother and I and our businesses."

"That is correct." No sense BS-ing a BS-er.

"With your permission, I can show her how to add another level of encryption. The government is always a step behind private enterprise. That way, her avatar is completely cloaked."

"I'll pass it along," I tell him. The mention of my daughter in the same sentence as the cops is not upsetting me. Multi-millionaires looking to stay below the radar don't get that way by being careless.

"I understand your interest in the deaths of your former students, especially because of the lackluster response by law enforcement. One was made to look like a death by suicide, and the other an accident."

"It's no secret that is what I think," I reply.

He stops, so I turn to look at him. "I agree with you," he says, "and that is why I want you to keep investigating. How can I help you?"

I am not expecting that curve ball, and he catches me flat-footed. "I not sure you can," I tell him.

"Why? Because you suspect us of the killings? That is a reasonable question, isn't it? Yes, we dealt with the body shop, and our preference to use cash raised some eyebrows and caused some differences between the partners, but everything got worked out. Business was returning to normal."

"I see," I say, and I resume walking. He catches up with me.

"I mean, we can't give you any money or be obvious about it, but I have more faith in you finding the real killer or killers than in Officer Williams or Detective Shafer."

"They have talked to you?" I ask.

"Not yet. Eventually somebody will. I'd like for you to make that an unnecessary task for us to have to go through."

"I am trying to wrap my head around this conversation, Simon."

"It's simple, Mrs. Strong. My brother and I do not have a strong alibi on the night of the Dawson shooting, we were home watching a movie—"

"The Rambo movie?" I ask.

"Yes, how did you know?"

"The same reason gangsters have the lines to *Goodfellas* memorized, I guess."

He smiles. "But for the Yelito death, we may have been the last persons to see him alive before the killer."

"You picked up the gas tank?"

"Right again, Mrs. Strong. He called us to come and pick it up. We didn't have another and would have to order one."

"About what time was that?"

He holds out a CD. "This is from the ATM camera of the bank across the street from the auto body. Our arrival and departure times are date and time stamped. Yelito is seen moving another car around on the lot after we left."

"Have the police seen this yet?" I ask.

"No, we do some serious banking there, and they did us a favor. I made something up about thinking one of our vehicles was vandalized across the street and we wanted to check it out."

"A little white lie."

"Yes, but we thought about it, and the cops didn't. What does that tell you?"

I turn the corner to see the market a block away. "You had nothing to do with Jake or Brian's death." I am back to zero suspects now, and I must find another motive for their deaths.

"That is correct."

"But by us pointing out the Mustang to Shafer, the police are looking at the two of you now and you would rather the police not know your business."

"Exactly."

"Or the government."

"Especially the government." That is his real issue; two local murders are not.

"The sooner the real killer or killers are caught, the sooner the heat is off the Stillman brothers," I summarize for him.

He shrugs at the obvious conclusion. "There is another vehicle arriving and departing before you return to the shop, Mrs. Strong. We can't make out the license plate or the driver, I am afraid."

He extends the CD to me, and I take it. "The enemy of my enemy is my friend, huh, Simon?" I look him square in the eyes.

"Couldn't have said it better myself," he replies. "After you shop, we can give you a ride home if you'd like."

"That is very nice of you, Simon, but I need to think about your proposal."

"Well, your daughter knows about a dozen ways to contact

us." He smiles and walks back to the street we were just on, and that same shiny truck stops to pick him up.

I text Erin. *Call me when you can, new developments in our case.*

Will do is her reply.

Just as I reach the door, my cell dings again. She sent me a song. I put in my ear buds. Steven Tyler's voice pounds my temples as he sings Aerosmith's "Back in the Saddle." I swear she can read my mind sometimes.

CHAPTER TWENTY-ONE

An old laptop that I couldn't throw away has a disk drive on it. The operating system is so old that it won't allow me to download the app to play the video. I could have asked Ken to pick up a CD drive to attach to my new laptop, but I receive a better offer.

April, my youngest granddaughter, is on my lap. Jesse, Erin's middle daughter, is drawing dinosaurs in a coloring book next to me, and her oldest, Caleb, is in the attic with Ken and my son-in-law, Darren. We don't ask, but they are doing something with power tools. Erin has played the footage through at various speeds on her screaming fast machine, using the same app the FBI uses, but not until she had scanned the disc for viruses and malware. Wouldn't it be fun if the Stillmans gave us something that captures every keystroke, turns the camera and microphones on and off, or erases all the data on the machine and sends the virus off to the FBI's server firewalls? Erin said that to me before I could do anything really stupid. My words, not hers. I won't be firing up that old laptop again. It's going into the town dump on Monday.

"It's a black Honda Accord, about ten years old, give or take a few years," she tells me.

"Is that good?" I ask.

"No, and yes. That particular model took turns with Toyota's Corolla being the most popular car sold at the time in America."

"That doesn't help us. What's the good news?" I ask.

"It narrows down the field of people who know Jake or Brian or have business with them."

"I'll keep my eyes peeled, Watson," I tell her. We take turns playing Dr. Watson and the smart-ass he shared rooms with on Baker Street.

"The car enters slowly at two forty-four, stays for about fifteen minutes, and exits quickly. We never see the driver." She marks the timeline on my chalkboard. Thank goodness I didn't erase the first one. Two murders with two timelines. In for a penny, in for a pound. "How long before your father and I show up?" I ask.

"The Accord departs at two fifty-eight, and you and daddy arrive at four-fifteen."

"Hold on, Honey," I tell her. I swing April onto my hip, and we go up to the attic.

"Caleb is learning how to use a power sander," I tell her upon my return. I hand her Ken's phone, and she pulls up the voice message. She notes the time of the call as 2:19 p.m. She sends the message to her phone and then emails it from her phone to her laptop and places it in the *Dawson* folder.

"I'd love to get his cellphone records," she says.

"I could circle back with Candace to see if Jake and Brian expensed their cellphones through the business."

"Earlier, you leave at two-eleven on foot, and eight minutes later he's leaving you a message on Dad's phone saying that he forgot to tell you something." She adds this to the timeline with notations.

"Makes sense. He had a few minutes to think about what we talked about, and since he didn't know how to reach me, he had to get Ken's number and then left him a message."

"But it's the way he said it, Mom."

We listen again.

"You're right, Erin. He knows he's leaving a message on my husband's business cell phone."

"He's referring to a private conversation he had with you that Daddy wouldn't know anything about."

I think aloud. "Otherwise, he would have just said, 'I forgot to tell you X, Mrs. Strong.'"

"He was expecting you to call him back. Maybe there was more that he wanted to say to you once he had you on the phone."

"Your father gave me the message as soon as he got home."

"You tried calling him a little after four." She looks at my phone's call log and notes the exact time on the timeline."

"By that time, Brian was under the car."

"What was he doing under the car, Mommy?" Jesse asks without looking up from the purple triceratops.

If both Erin and I showed up to ask him one question, Barney Williams would feel like he is being double-teamed. He's leaning on his cruiser, intently listening to something on his cellphone's tethered headphones. This rare Saturday appearance of Officer Williams is due to signal repairs on one of the town's few traffic signals. Everybody has to treat the flashing red lights like the intersection is controlled by stop signs.

I walk around in front of him to get his attention, after calling his name several times. I can hear the country rock leaking from his ears three feet away. "Hi, Barney."

"Hi, Mrs. Strong. What's up?"

"It was something Mike Strohmeyer told me. He said I should talk to you. Just a quick question if you are not too busy, officer." I smile. I can play nice when I have to.

"What is it?" His curiosity is roused by my referencing a county sheriff.

"Sharon McGrath and Jake Dawson had been dating since before high school, but Mike said that Jake might have had a side girlfriend."

He nodded his head.

"It wouldn't look good for Jake if Sharon found out about her at their wedding. Trying to think of a reason he'd do that to himself rather than get married," I tell him. I can't read his eyes or facial expression, mostly because he is wearing aviator reflector sunglasses.

"He was parked down by the river a couple of months ago. I lit him up with the headlights and the searchlight." He pats the searchlight that he can maneuver from a swivel inside of his cruiser. "It took him a few seconds to put his pants on, and he came out of his truck and met me halfway between our vehicles. That's when I recognized him. He was sober and scared that I would see the girl. He was straight up with me and said that it wasn't his fiancée."

"Yes, that's right. It wasn't Sharon," I agree.

"I told him I had to make sure that his passenger was safe. I told him that guys sometimes take advantage of passed out girls or they fed them date-rape drugs."

"Makes sense to me," I say.

"Then from his truck, I hear her say, 'I'm okay, Barney, we aren't doing anything wrong.' I look at Jake and he's petrified that I will see who he's with. There is something called 'officer's discretion.' There are times when what's going on is none of my business. No laws being broken. Usually, it's underage kids drinking or doing drugs I encounter down there.

He's not drunk, and I don't think the woman is in any kind of danger."

"I can understand that. Some people can't get the privacy they want when they really need it."

"I told Jake that it would be a good idea if he left before me."

"And?"

"He did."

"And the girl?" There is the question that I had to wait to ask until now.

"Wasn't one hundred percent sure who it was."

"But you had an idea," I proffer.

"Yeah, she tried raising her voice higher than normal, but I've heard it before."

I wait. I want to ask, but he can refuse me. It is better to create the tension for him wanting to tell me.

The cherry picker with the traffic signal repairperson lowers from above the intersection. The signals are now red for the cross street and green for the main thoroughfare. We watch the traffic signals go about their normal change routines of green, yellow and red. The work site will be no longer when the worker gets out of the basket.

Barney gets the thumbs up from the worker. He can leave now. He shuffles his girth into the cruiser and rearranges his police utility belt holding all his toys. I am committed to waiting him out. His need to tell me must be greater than my curiosity. He radios into communications and waits for their acknowledgement. He sets the microphone back on the console. He presses the button to roll down his window. I move closer to his open window.

"I think someday it might come in handy for me," he says.

"Oh?"

He looks in all his rear-view windows and leans towards me. "Vickie Scudder."

"The mayor's daughter?"

"Yep, she's over eighteen, and I wasn't about to check out how much clothing she had on. Telling the mayor what she was doing down by the river with Jake wouldn't win me any points and if I rousted them, the mayor might take sides. I like my job, Mrs. Strong. On the other hand, I might be able to call in a favor with Vickie someday."

"That was very smart of you, Barney," I say truthfully.

"I didn't tell anybody the girl's name until now. I know that you won't tell her I told you."

"It's our secret. The death by suicide angle makes more sense if Jake was afraid that Vickie was to make a scene at the church."

The I-told-you-so look on his face doesn't need further explanation.

I continue. "I have one last thing to do before stopping poking around on this case, Barney. Would you have a problem if I talked to Becky Steele? She might have more to say about Jake. She was there that night with Brian."

"I don't see any harm in that, Mrs. Strong, if it helps you satisfy yourself."

"Thanks, Barney."

The utility truck and his cruiser ease away. Once out of sight, Erin comes up to me. "What did our friendly constable have to say, Mom?"

"He drove down by the river and spotted a truck parked at night. Jake came out, pulling up his pants and said that he didn't want Barney to see who he was with." We walk in the other direction towards home.

"I take it that it wasn't Sharon."

"He didn't see the woman Jake was with, but he thinks by her voice that she is the Mayor's youngest, Vickie."

"Oh my. The plot thickens."

"He said that she tried disguising her voice and said she was all right. He chose not to pursue it, as nothing good would come out of it if she decided to tell her father that the cop was harassing her. Barney thinks that I am buying into the official cause of death ruling. Not sure what he and Shafer are finding out about the Stillman twins. I didn't want to push my luck. He understood that I wasn't interested in butting heads with him. He didn't have a problem with me talking to Becky Steele about the night Jake died."

"It's better to look like you are not pursuing the deaths," she tells me.

"Healthier too," I reply.

"Speaking of healthier, what are you planning for dinner tomorrow night?"

"The usual Sunday night fare. Yankee pot roast, mashed potatoes, green beans, salad, and a cobbler with ice cream."

"You will get no complaints from my bunch," she says.

"Can you ask your brother to join us? When was the last time he saw his nieces and nephew?"

"A couple of weeks ago. He stops by all the time," Erin tells me.

It's a little disarming that he finds the time to be a doting uncle. "Well, I haven't seen my baby boy since the Fourth of July fireworks celebration. Please ask him. I don't want to nag him," I say.

We get home, and Darren has my adorable grandchildren belted into their car seats. I kiss each one goodbye, and Ken and I wave goodbye to them. Then I fill him in on Barney's revelation without mentioning the mayor's daughter. I tell him that I have a couple more interviews to finish on the auto body owners' deaths over the weekend. I want him to think that I am coasting to the finish line. Part of it is true, part is for show. I don't want to alarm him further and am trying to fly below the radar; a quote my father is fond of saying.

CHAPTER TWENTY-TWO

It's Sunday morning before church. Those are not words that I usually put together in a sentence, but I have a plan for today. I am walking on this clear, crisp morning to see Sharon McGrath. Then, after attending the normal Sunday church service, I am going to ask Becky Steele to give me a ride to the graveside memorial service for Brian Yelito.

There was no viewing for Brian, and a short remembrance at the gravesite is the only thing the now-divorced parents could agree on. They've not asked me to get involved with his death. I have no regrets about pushing Shafer and Barney to treat his death as a homicide. I will talk with them after the service separately if I can.

I zigzag on streets and alleys to Sharon's apartment, where she is expecting me. "Hello Mrs. Strong, How are you?" she says when I arrive.

"Thanks for seeing me on such short notice."

She hands me a mug of coffee. "It's not like I am doing anything else. We were supposed to fly home today from our honeymoon and then we would have been back to work tomorrow."

The reality of Jake's death and returning to her normal routine tomorrow without him is clear as she moves listlessly around her apartment. She's still in her sweatpants and an oversized T-shirt that hasn't seen a washing machine since before Jake died. She didn't wash her hair yet today, and I will say nothing about her personal hygiene.

I still have trouble wrapping my head around her, going from a bride-to-be to grieving the loss of her best friend, yet I am here to ask her a few delicate questions.

"Sharon, did you and Jake share a phone plan?"

"No, he and Brian had one through the business. It was a write-off."

"Okay, I will talk to Candace about getting the call and text records. It would not be uncommon for a bookkeeper to ask for those things, especially since she paid the bills."

Sharon cocks her head.

I add, "The records might give me more to work with, especially since Brian died."

"I heard that you and Mr. Strong found him."

"Yes, we did. I had talked to him earlier in the day at the body shop, and he called Ken and left a message that he had something else to tell me."

"I guess you will never know what was on his mind," she says.

"No, but by Brian not answering his phone, I went back to the shop and found him dead. I made sure the police would look at the scene as a crime scene and not as an accident."

"Is that what you think, that Brian was murdered?" she asks.

"I do. Just as still think that Jake didn't have a reason to kill himself."

She stirs her coffee vigorously and stares into the swirling vortex. I have to take her down into an equally dark place now.

"I have to ask you a question for which I have a partial

answer. Did Jake step out on you in the months before you two were to be married?"

She looks up without surprise and says evenly, "Yes."

"Do you know with whom?"

"No. Do you?" she asks me.

I do not answer but instead answer her question with a question. "Would you have been surprised if some other women objected to your marriage to Jake during the ceremony?"

"No."

I am taken aback by that answer and need some clarification. I sip my coffee and wait as I look into her eyes. Why don't you dig the knife in a little deeper, Gwen?

"When I was away at college, I cheated on him. I wanted to be sure that he was the one for me. I told him after I graduated. I didn't go into the details of how many guys or what I did with them, but I was honest with him. I told him I got it out of my system. I was positive that he was my real love."

"Okay." I say the only thing I can think of while I wait for the other shoe to drop.

"He came to me later and said that he had a few flings too, and that the girls meant nothing to him. I guess as we got closer to the date, he admitted to succumbing to a few lapses in his promise to be faithful. He said that if I wanted to call off the wedding, I could. He said that I could even keep the engagement ring."

"And?"

"In the end, I forgave him, and he promised that from then on and in our marriage, he would not fool around again. Getting the second chance made him realize how much he loved me. If some bimbo showed up at our wedding to talk sh—garbage, we would have been prepared for it. I would be surprised who it was, but it wouldn't have mattered. No, Mrs. Strong, Jake didn't kill himself because he didn't want to get married."

"And he wasn't afraid if some other woman objected to your marriage?"

"No. We could handle it. If somebody did that, they would be the one looking a little foolish."

"Thank you, Sharon. I know that wasn't easy for you," I say and without missing a beat, I add, "Was there anything with the Stillman twins that he was holding back from you that you think now made it so terrible that he had no way out but to end his life?"

"Absolutely not. He had no secrets with me about his work. Do you think they killed him?"

I reply, "If they killed both Jake and Brian and made one to look like a death by suicide and the other to be an accident, they would have to have a pretty good motive."

"They are not people to mess with, Mrs. Strong. I know that much."

"I don't think they killed the boys, but I pointed the cops in their direction at first."

"Then who did kill them?" she asks me.

I look out her kitchen window to the street below as I compose my answer carefully. "At first, I thought that Brian had motive to kill Jake over their disagreements about the Stillman twins paying cash under the table and Brian being the beneficiary of a large life insurance policy that each partner had taken out on the other."

"And?" It was Sharon's turn to ply me for more information.

"Then I talked to Brian, and I thought there was no way he could do such a thing. He wasn't even aware of the life insurance policy amounts and said that he and Jake were cool with the Stillman twins."

"I didn't know about the life insurance policies," she tells me.

"Candace told me that the business was paying the premiums for several years. Each policy had a million-dollar payout."

"Wow!" Sharon almost spits out a mouthful of coffee.

"Pretty strong motive to start your own business and use Vo-Tech kids to fill in until Brian could hire the best graduates," I say.

She nods. "I still don't see it. Those two guys were inseparable. Brian could not plan to make a murder look like a death by suicide of his best friend over money. No way, Mrs. Strong."

"You knew them better as adults than I did, but I watched them grow up, and I came to the same conclusion after talking to Brian," I tell her.

"How do you figure Brian's death?" she asks me.

I tell her, "I looked hard at the Stillman twins wanting to make a clean break from Jake and Brian, but then I got evidence that showed the twins couldn't have killed Brian."

"You did?"

"They visited the shop right after I did. I figured Brian called them, but then someone else visited the shop before I returned there later that afternoon. He was still alive when they left the shop, Sharon. They don't want anybody knowing their business. They are up to something, but I don't know what it is. I am pretty sure it was not enough to kill the boys."

"So, where are you with things now?"

"I feel stronger that Jake didn't kill himself and that Brian's death was not an accident, and the two are tied together. I will keep asking around."

She shakes her head. "In the end, they both are dead, and nothing will bring them back, but knowing what happened is important to me, even if it's getting the cloud from over my head that Jake killed himself the day before he was to marry me."

I have enough time if I hurry to get to the ten o'clock service. I say, "You know everything I can tell you, Sharon. I appreciate you telling me the truth about you and Jake. It makes the death by suicide motive less plausible."

I get up to leave, and she stands up and away from the table. We hug.

I reach for the door handle and feel like Columbo when I say, "There's one other thing. Do you know anybody who drives a ten-year-old black Honda Accord?"

She tells me.

I didn't see that coming.

I'm sure that Jeremiah Steele is a wonderful preacher and that the choristers sing like angels, but all of that is lost on me as I ponder the piece of evidence that was just handed to me. What makes it more difficult is figuring how to go about using it. I can't go upstairs into the loft of the church and secretly text Erin. I am in this alone, and I will not blow it. There is the fact that a car of that vintage and color was the most popular car produced a decade ago. I don't know how many people in our small town own one. What reason would many of them have to visit Brian? That cuts down the list. Then there is the one person who Sharon knows who owns one. That person knows Brian and would have reasons to visit him.

I accept the invitation to stay for coffee hour. I am chatting with parents of former students when I decide to slip off to the bathroom. I am not used to drinking that much coffee. I open the door to the bathroom as Becky Steele emerges.

"Hi, Mrs. Strong, how did you like the service?"

"Warm and welcoming," I reply. "Good words to hear after what we've gone through in the last couple of weeks."

"Amen," she replies. "The community is hurting after losing two of their own."

I am puzzled by her distancing her own feelings about what happened to Jake and Brian. "I was hoping to talk with you a bit,

Becky. I need a ride to the cemetery. Could I go with you? Maybe we could talk on the way?"

Standing in the hallway between the chatter during coffee hour and the flushing toilets of the rest rooms, she is comfortable in this building, a structure that is like a second home to her. She smiles easily. "Sure, I also want to talk to you too, Mrs. Strong."

We both return to the coffee hour, and Jeremiah pulls me to the side. "Good morning, Gwen. It is nice to see you this morning."

He's asking without saying it out loud why I am here. "It's sad that Brian Yelito's family didn't ask you to preside over a memorial service."

"Everyone grieves differently. I offered, but his family couldn't decide what to do," Steele says.

"Well, I needed to have some time with my thoughts today before going to the cemetery and want to thank you for a wonderful service."

"You've taken quite an interest in your former students, I've heard," he says.

"How so?"

"I don't know any teachers that go to where their students died and question the authorities."

"Thank you, Jeremiah, for your response, but I wanted to know how you heard." If he had told me how he heard, I would have asked him what he heard. I am getting better at this sort of questioning, and from his reaction, he is not accustomed to being put on the spot.

"Gwen, you know as well as I do this is a small town. People talk."

"People?" I know I am pushing him now.

He doesn't answer me and instead tries to circle back to his original theme. "Don't you think it's best to let the professionals do what they are trained to do?"

"Why is that?" I won't budge. I don't care that I am in the basement of his house of worship.

"Because they don't make wild assertions."

"Like?"

"That somehow Jake didn't take his life."

"Don't forget Brian. We don't want to assume that his death was an accident, either."

"That's exactly what I am talking about. Death by suicides and accidents are unfortunate events, but they happen."

"I agree, Reverend Steele, and so do premeditated murders, even in a small town like Milford, unless you feel that not one of the flock could be a wolf in sheep's clothing."

I can see he is struggling with how much he wants to enter a battle of wits with me. I get the sense that Reverend Jeremiah Steele likes to get the last word in.

Quoting from scripture, he tries to gain the upper hand, saying, "Jesus answered the disciples that many cannot see or hear the truth because of their stubborn hearts."

"I agree with you wholeheartedly. Why do the 'people' that talked to you cling to that version of events"

Just then I see Becky trying to catch my eye, and before he can reach into his magic bag of tricks quoting from the Greek or Hebrew translations, I end with, "I'm going to Brian's memorial and see what else I can discern regarding the truth about his death."

CHAPTER TWENTY-THREE

Once I am belted into Becky's car and we depart the church property, she says, "Not many people talk to my father like that, Mrs. Strong."

"Why's that, Becky?" I am getting a kick out of answering questions with a question today.

"He's part of the God squad. How can you argue with someone who spouts scripture at you?"

I remind myself to ask her if she feels she is swimming in a fishbowl, but that will be for another time and place. "I never backed down from authority figures before. Why would I change now?" I shrug. "Sometimes I had to stand my ground when I knew it was best for the kids, you know?"

She plows ahead with what she wants to say. "I want to apologize for the way I acted at the Dawson home after the burial. I was sleep deprived. I had drunk too much that weekend and felt terrible about the whole situation."

I say quickly, "I apologize too, for assuming you and Sharon talked after Jake died. I have learned from all this that people grieve differently." A silence ensues. I'm all about listening to what Becky wants to tell me.

"And then look what happened to Brian," she says.

"I know. I am the one that discovered him."

"That's right," she says as we turn into the cemetery. "I am so sorry that you had to see him that way. Why did you go to the body shop, Mrs. Strong?"

I bite my tongue when I am tempted to ask, *What way is that?* "As you know, I don't have a car, and since he owned a body shop, I thought he might know of someone wanting to sell a used car, or he could keep an eye out for one that he could fix up for me. I am not walking to school anymore and we need a second car. Don't you think that makes sense?" I lie to her, and I know that she knows I am lying. I am happy to tweak her.

"Uh, sure. You are looking for a second car now. I get it."

"Say, Becky. This car rides nice. What kind of car is it?"

"A Honda Accord."

"Do you like it?"

"It was a hand-me-down from my parents."

"How old is it?"

"I dunno."

"It's real comfortable. Do you think they make them in other colors? Black is not one of my favorites."

"I'm sure they do." She shoots a sideways look at me.

I am going to hitch a ride from Candace back home from the service. The sunshine and warm air make for a pleasant afternoon, except for the fact a small town is burying one of their own. A death of a young person is hard. So much promise. Everyone knows the family, and many locals are here to pay their respects.

Candace and I talk at the gravesite when the service concludes. She tells me the former Mrs. Yelito was gone before she could offer any condolences. I don't tell her what I have planned, other than asking for the business phone records from her. I must be very careful where I go next. There is a killer afoot.

Everybody grieves differently is what I told Becky earlier. That is apparent today with Brian's mom. Whatever she is feeling, she is not about to share it with the fine folks of Milford, a town she fled a decade ago. Out of habit, I am about to blame my mother for fleeing England, but I hitch up my big girl pants and remember there is more to the story. Someday, I might hear it from her. I might find out from Brian's mom why she left right after the divorce.

Detective Shafer and I nod to each other. He doesn't approach me, and I know I'm not about to poke the bear again. Too much is at stake now. Just him being here lets me know he is taking my thoughts seriously.

Brian's father and his stepmother are in no condition to talk to me. *Gee, guess what guys, you are about to receive a life insurance payout of a million dollars, maybe two, if your son's death is ruled an accident under the double indemnity provisions of the policies for accidental death. But that is not the case. I think he was murdered. Oh, as an aside, I suspected your son of killing his best friend, but I don't anymore. Sorry for your loss.*

I mill about, chatting with former students and some of their parents. Mike Strohmeyer must have told Yvette about our private chat, and they stay their distance. That girl better deliver this week. She looks so uncomfortable being this overdue.

I recall the photo I have tacked up in my office. Three kids from that class are now dead. The other died on his high school graduation night from choking on his own puke in his sleep after chugging a bottle of whiskey on a dare. Most of their classmates are here today. There is no doubt about the bonds formed in a small town.

The LeGrande clan is early for dinner. I haven't heard if Wesley will honor us with his presence. I go upstairs and lay my skirt and blouse on the bed, then change into slacks and a comfy top. Erin and I talk about the case as we prepare the traditional Strong Sunday dinner. Ken and Darren are kicking the ball around with the kids in the backyard.

I spill about Becky driving a black Honda Accord. It sets Erin's wheels spinning.

"She and Brian discover Jake's death shortly after it happened, and she is probably the last person to see Brian alive."

"And now Brian is dead," I add.

"And now Brian is dead," she repeats.

"Don't forget, the maid of honor has yet to talk to the bride-to-be about what she saw that night at the cabin," I say.

"She tells the grapevine that Jake would rather shoot himself than marry Sharon," she adds.

"What's that all mean to you?" I place the roast in the oven as Erin mashes the potatoes.

"And you don't like the Stillman twins for this?" She's asking herself as much as me.

"Instead of warning me off, the smart one, Simon, tells me to keep digging. I am convinced that they are up to no good, but it doesn't include killing the boys. He doesn't want the cops sniffing around and stumbling upon whatever they are really doing."

We watch from the kitchen window as our husbands and my adorable grandchildren run around chasing a soccer ball while we mull over the recent developments.

"Abe from the yoga studio said that I was called to this work," I tell her.

"I'm the apple and you are the tree, Mom. If I hadn't dragged you to New Haven last year, we might never have discovered your gift. I think we have to see what the telephone records are going to tell us."

"Telephone records?"

We turn to see my baby boy, who is all grown up now.

"Wesley, you made it!" I say.

"Erin said that I had to. You had something to ask me."

I look at Erin with a puzzled look.

She says, "The fishbowl."

"Right. Can I get you anything to drink?" I ask.

"Your sweet, iced tea would be nice," he says.

We retreat to the kitchen. He takes his seat where his highchair once rested. He is taller than both Erin and Ken and looks to have added some heavy weights to his exercise regimen. He and I are darker than Erin. Don't ask me to explain the genetics of biracial marriages. His black hair is cut short, while mine is still in the soft Afro I've worn since before they were born. No gray yet. It allows me to tweak Ken when I tug on his silver-haired temples, reminding him he is older than me.

I pour and talk. "One of my old students commented about Becky Steele growing up in a fishbowl because her father is a well-known pastor in a small town." I push the glass over to Wesley's placemat. "She said that you and Erin would feel that way because I was a schoolteacher in town."

"Never had to do with you being a schoolteacher, Mom," he says as he takes a long pull.

"What then?" Erin asks.

"Maybe people said nothing to you guys being part-Black, but it didn't stop the kids from saying what their parents thought to me."

I look at Erin.

Erin shakes her head. "I remember nothing like that. I was the first girl in my class to have boobs, and that interested the boys more than anything else."

I smile at her and shake my head. "What else, Wes?"

"Not being white in an almost completely white small town wasn't easy, but they thought I was gay, too."

"And?" I ask. This is new ground for my son and me, but glancing at Erin, I think they've had this conversation before.

He looks at me, sets his glass down, then steals a look at Erin and says, "I didn't want to explore my feelings here in town, but it was easier at school where nobody cared."

That might explain his reserved demeanor and shyness all those years. "And?"

"After I graduated, I still enjoy living in a college town where there are young people from all over the world. What I do and who I do it with is nobody's business. It's more relaxing."

Just then, April comes running in from the yard and screams, "Uncle Wesley!" She throws herself into his waiting arms, and he lifts her in a practiced move into the air above his head.

"Hey, baby girl." He then blows baby kisses into her belly, and she giggles. They've done this before, I suspect.

He looks to me over her head, finally coming up for air, and says, "I will let you know before I bring anyone over for dinner. Okay?"

Maybe this is why both Erin and Ken said I had to ask Wesley what it was like swimming in a fishbowl of a small town.

Erin and I can put aside our musings about Jake and Brian's death as Caleb and Jesse erupt into the house followed by our two out-of-breath husbands.

Dinner was a success. I kiss both my children and my son-in-law goodbye. I give extra kisses to my grandchildren. Ken and I talk about our day and what we are planning in the upcoming week as we do the dishes.

I am first upstairs and spot my skirt and blouse on the bed. I inspect them to decide if I can get another wear out of them or if they must go to the dry cleaners. The blouse definitely has to go, but as I look at the skirt, I notice some things that static electricity has attached to the fabric which covers my bottom. I look closer and realize what they are. I go into the bathroom and retrieve my tweezers. I call down to Ken to bring me up a baggie. He doesn't ask why until I tell him what I think they are and where they came from.

Then I wait an hour for Erin and Darren to put the kids to bed before I call her. We examine our separate copies of the crime scene photos we took at the cabin when we talk and curse that we didn't take more photos. We have to get back in that cabin.

CHAPTER TWENTY-FOUR

Thoughts do not bubble up during my meditation and yoga this Monday morning. I can focus on my breath and my postures. Maybe it was because I spent half the night on the living room couch, turning like a speared piece of meat on a rotisserie. The excitement of the breakthrough lasted until the sun rose, and I am exhausted.

I am quiet as I help Emelina and Abe put things away. I don't feel the need to discuss the crime scene photos and why goose feathers are so important to solving the case. We enjoy a comfortable silence, mostly because I am not longing to question my calling. I see Ken in the doorway.

"Hi, Abe, how's the studio?" he asks

"Great, Ken. Let me know when you are ready to talk about finishing the upstairs."

"If you've got some time now, I can go out and grab my notepad and tape measure."

"By all means," Abe says.

"Two other things," Ken says. "Just a reminder, Emelina, I can help you out with some fall chores. Your chocolate chip cookies are the best I've ever tasted. I'm sure we can barter something." He has a twinkle in his eyes. I love that man.

She beams at my husband. "Are you sure? You will do a lot of work for my cookies."

Everyone is smiling, then Ken says, "Turn your phone on, hon. Erin's been trying to reach you since eight o'clock."

"Is it the kids?"

He coughs and says, "No, it's about that thing you and she are working on." He doesn't know how much I share with Abe and Emelina.

I make a beeline for my bag, and as I turn the phone on, I tell him, "I'll walk you out to the truck."

We get outside, then Ken says, "She didn't know what else to do, so she called me. I waited until I saw other people leaving."

"Thanks. Do you mind if I sit in your truck while I talk to her?"

"Not at all. Abe and I won't be long."

"Indoor work is great work when it turns cold outside." I repeat what he often says.

He gives me a peck on the cheek as grabs his pad and tape.

Thank goodness, I don't have to hold my breath waiting for my phone to turn on. It's an older model that I've dropped only a few times, but I can still read the screen through the fissures.

"Hi Erin, what's up that you had to send Daddy after me?"

"You guys didn't watch the news this morning?" she asks.

"No, I don't care about traffic, and I can stick my head out the window for the weather. We like to start our day off with a minimum of excitement, honey."

"Well, your day just got a hell of a lot more exciting. Caleb, go back in the dining room. Grammy Strong and I have to talk for a few minutes." There is a pause. "He thinks that every time I go into the kitchen, he's going to get something to eat. He's like a puppy, I swear." I can hear her moving to the counter where she keeps her iPad. "The State Police arrested Jason Stillman early this morning on charges of murdering both Jake Dawson and Brian Yelito. As best as I can tell, they are saying the motive has to do with stolen cars."

I am stunned.

"Mom? Are you there?"

"Yes."

"What are you thinking?"

"I'm thinking that Simon Stillman played me."

"How so?"

"He wanted me to keep looking into it and create, create…"

"Reasonable doubt."

"That's the phrase, reasonable doubt. He could not influence the investigation directly, so he encouraged me to keep going, and he gave us that CD to prove their innocence in Brian's death."

"And Jake?"

"No defense there, as they could not establish an alibi."

"How do you feel?" she asks me.

"I don't really know. It doesn't add up to me. We talked about what we needed to do. We have to get back inside the cabin and then talk to Sharon one more time."

"There's more, Mom. They identified the gun that killed Jake as being owned by Jason Stillman."

My mind races back to finding the extra clip of ammunition in Jake's dresser. "We always assumed that Jake owned the gun that killed him. That's another thing to talk to Sharon about. Where did the gun come from?"

"The FBI, ATF, and the State Police raided their place in the woods outside of town before dawn this morning. Best I can tell, it is off a logging trail. The aerial photos show a couple of those prepper containers attached end to end. They hauled a bunch of guns out of there, too. Somebody tipped the local TV station, so they had a reporter up there as the sun came up. This is big news. Two homicides cleared and survivalists stashing lots of guns."

"Two local kids working hard to make a living didn't want to play ball with the Stillman twins, and when they threatened to end the relationship, they got killed." I shake my head. "Brian, Sharon, or Candace would have said something to me if things had gotten that serious. It just doesn't add up," I repeat.

"What are you saying, Mom? You turned the police onto the Stillman twins. You argued with Detective Shafer and Barney Williams that Jake didn't kill himself and that Brian's death was not an accident."

"Are the cops saying there was more about the Mustangs between the twins and the boys that nobody knew about?" I ask my daughter. She spends more time on true crime TV shows and podcasts than anybody else I know. Both of our wheels are spinning now.

"I have to check on the kids, Mom. Let me think about it."

"Love 'em and hug 'em. We can circle back after I talk to Candace and Sharon, but I am telling you, it doesn't sit right with me."

"Love you, Mommy."

"Love you too, honey."

Ken comes back to the truck with a smile on his face. "Abe is not only talking about rehabbing upstairs, but he wants to expand the kitchen and bring in commercial grade appliances. I think Emelina is going to make lots of cookies here."

"She's over a hundred years old," I say in astonishment.

"She wants to pass on the recipes. She's not getting any younger is what she told Abe."

I think about my mentor and how she has more energy than people half her age. "Do you think you can drop me off at Emory's Auto Parts? I need to talk with Candace Dawson."

"Okay. What did Erin want to talk about?"

"The State Police raided the Stillman's place out in the woods, confiscated a bunch of guns, and arrested Jason Stillman for the murders of Jake and Brian."

"That's fantastic, Gwen. You made them look closer at both deaths."

We pull from the curb. He U-turns at the next four-way stop and heads back towards the main street in town. I say nothing.

"That is a good thing, isn't it?" I can tell he's saying it as much for himself out of relief that I will be out of harm's way as he is happy for me.

My tired brain is flooded with thoughts and emotions slapping at me like ocean waves at high tide. We stop in front of Emory's, and I say to him, "Remember last year, when Erin and I went to that true crime symposium where the cops had botched the initial investigation?"

"Of course. What are you saying, sweetie?" He looks at me with a puzzled grin.

"It feels the same."

Ken's smile vanishes as he stares out the windshield.

Candace confesses, "I didn't want to say anything at Brian's gravesite yesterday, Mrs. Strong, but the police asked me who the boy's phone carrier was on Friday. They were going to subpoena the records."

"Can I still ask you for them?" I ask.

"Why? You got the police to re-investigate Jakes's death, and they made an arrest." She munches on a snack bar. I caught her just as she is taking a mid-morning break at her desk, and I am told fifteen minutes is all I have.

I honestly don't have an acceptable answer for her now. *Gee,*

Candace. I think the cops acted too quickly and I am not sure they arrested the right person. "I was just curious about a few things, and it would help me with the timeline, that's all." It's the best I can do.

"You still want to look into this. Why?" She has a skeptical look on her face.

"I don't think everything I was told by some of the witnesses was truthful, and I want to know who might have been lying to me."

She flushes red at me. "You said that Jake didn't kill himself. We now know who killed him thanks to you pushing the cops to take a harder look. Why do you want to upset the apple cart?"

I am talking to a sister who just buried her baby brother, and she is desperately seeking closure. "You're right, Candace. I should leave it to the professionals now. Just one other thing. Did you know that Jake had a handgun?"

"No, I didn't. He stopped hunting the day after he got his first buck. He never wanted to kill another thing after that day. I never knew him to own a gun."

Sharon is taking a break from work. It's been a rough morning for her. She started early, then her phone blew up with calls and texts about the arrest. Her hands tremble as she sets a cup of herbal tea down for me.

"I asked him about the gun," she says, "and he told me that a customer gave it to him in trade. He said it was a relic from World War II."

"Where did he keep it?" I ask.

"In the top drawer of his dresser."

"Was it loaded?"

She nodded. "I grew up around guns in my parents' house, so it didn't bother me, having it there. It would be comforting, living out there on the edge of town when he worked late, knowing that I had some protection."

"Did he say who the customer was?"

She shook her head.

"I regret not asking Brian more about the Stillman twins when I had the chance," I say.

"Do you think that it would have changed anything?" she asks.

"Probably not, but I would have had a better answer to what the boys were involved in with the twins."

We both look out the window as we sip our cooling tea. Finally, she says to me, "Well, I am off the hook now. Jake didn't kill himself so as not to marry me."

"How does that make you feel?"

"I know my husband-to-be didn't commit death by suicide now. We always thought that, Mrs. Strong. It doesn't make the hurt go away, but at least we have closure. I don't have to wonder what was so terrible that he had to take his own life. Does that make sense?"

"It does, Sharon."

I get up to go. She gets up and hugs me. "Thank you for doing this. It means a lot to me."

I squeeze her back. I walk to the door and open it. A soft breeze wafts in. "Sharon, one other thing. Do you know what happened to Jake's pillow?"

"It should be still on the bed."

"Do you think Erin and I can borrow your key to look for it?"

She cocks her head. "Why, Mrs. Strong? They arrested Jason Stillman."

"It's just something I need to do. It's a loose end that I have to pick at."

MILFORD ELEMENTARY

She reaches to the board of eyehooks next to the door and slips a key off. "You can return it to Mabel and Warren. I won't be needing it anymore."

CHAPTER TWENTY-FIVE

Erin and I arrive before dark at Jake's cabin. The crime scene tape has been removed. Detective Shafer has his man.

Sharon's key still works, and we step into Jake's cabin, which still hasn't been cleaned up. The smell of dried blood is prevalent. I don't notice any changes. There is not a speck of fingerprint powder dusting any of the surfaces.

"They charge a guy for murder taking place inside a closed cabin and don't dust for prints?" Erin shakes her head in disgust.

"We've seen worse behavior." I am talking about the lack of crime scene investigation done in a dank apartment building stairwell where a young law student was brutally stabbed to death—the case we worked on last year. I look around the interior again and realize that the bed without a pillow called to me the last time I was here, but it was not until I saw the goose feathers on my skirt that I put it together. Goose feathers and no pillow are much of what Erin and I have to go on for a theory of what really happened that night.

The family will eventually have to pay someone to clean the blood from the table, wall, closed window, and floor if they plan to sell this place. I don't suspect that any of the Dawsons will want to live in the cabin now.

We photograph Jake's bed. We gently push the bed from the wall to make sure the pillow is not wedged there. There are no signs of a pillow anywhere in the house or in the trash cans outside.

I use my tweezers and baggies to collect the rest of the goose feathers I find in the dining room. There is not a single loose goose feather to be found on the bed, in the bathroom, or in the bedroom. Erin takes a video of me doing so. She had found some images online of the pillowcase that matched this NASCAR bedspread. She blew up images before we met up and printed some glossies. Fortunately, part of the pattern for the pillow matches the recurring pattern on the bedspread. I don't think that Jake will mind that I cut out a swatch of fabric. With a gloved hand, I use a butter knife to try to wedge open the dining room window that faces old Mr. Chalmers' property. The window doesn't budge, and that is a good sign. We depart quickly and start talking on the drive back to my house.

"Do you think Shafter will buy your theory?" Erin asks.

"Do you?" I reply.

"Even without seeing what the cops have, I can't say I agree with you, Mom."

"I still have a couple of things to do to tighten this up, but if I am right, they arrested the wrong person."

"I agree that if you kill someone with a gun, you don't leave it on the floor for the police to trace it back to you," she says.

"But you might if you want to make it look like a death by suicide," I add.

"You told me that Jason Stillman was not the one who got the brains when they were handed out that day."

I nod. "Simon reaching out to me is still bothersome, though."

"Unless it is exactly as it appears. Now that the police raided their hiding place, I think that it gives Simon more credence that he didn't want the cops looking into their other 'businesses.'"

My daughter is ambidextrous. She can drive and make air quotes at the same time. We turn the corner onto my street and see three vehicles idling across from our driveway. There is a shiny monster truck, a gleaming black Mercedes, and a non-descript sedan.

"Looks like you have company, Mom."

We pull into the driveway and wait a few beats as interior lights turn on from all three vehicles. Simon Stillman hops down from the truck. A woman in a sharp charcoal gray business suit emerges from the rear passenger seat of the Mercedes, and an older white male wearing a golf jacket over chinos follows behind her to the driveway entrance. They all stand there as Erin and I walk down the gravel drive to meet them.

"Mrs. Strong, this is Jason's attorney, Diane Rosenthal, and her private investigator, Bill Spencer."

I reach out my hand. "This is my daughter, Erin LeGrande. She works part-time for the FBI and might have a conflict if we are going to talk about Jason's predicament."

Attorney Rosenthal says, "Thank you for pointing that out. You are right. The FBI is involved in the investigation."

"I'm gonna head in and start dinner for you and Daddy," Erin says. She walks back to the house as Ken opens the door for her.

I wave to him and smile bravely. Turning back to the intrepid trio standing at the edge of our property, I say, "It's best that we talk out here. My husband doesn't need to hear this either."

"As you probably already know, Mrs. Strong, Jason was arrested this morning for the murder of Jake Dawson and Brian Yelito."

"Your client is up to something Attorney Rosenthal, but he did not kill those boys."

All their eyes widen, but only Simon has the courage to speak. "See? I told you we should talk to her."

"Simon, may I have a word with you in private?"

We walk away from my house and back in the direction whence Erin and I came. We are out of earshot of his high-priced hired talent. I say, "The Mustangs are not stolen. I am almost certain you are using them for another reason. Do I have your word that you will never come after me about the real purpose you had the boys working on those cars?"

"Yes," he gulps. "It was Jason's idea to use the cars."

"To be safe, I will leave an envelope in my bank deposit box with a statement about that, just in case. Are you okay with that?"

"Yes," he repeats.

"Good. I've only been asked to find out who killed Jake Dawson, and I feel responsible for getting Brian Yelito killed. I think I know who killed him, too. I need your help to prove it. You need to share as much as you can about the police investigation."

"Everything, Mrs. Strong, I promise."

"Okay." We shake on it. "There is no time to lose. I want to recreate the crime at the cabin tomorrow night." I jingle the key in front of him. "I just need to clear up three things in the morning."

I walk back to the attorney and the investigator and tell them what I need to prove my theory. Both, I am sure, want to tell me they know best, but Simon is paying them enough money to humor me. After about fifteen minutes, Erin signals me from the house. "Sorry, guys," I tell them. "If I knew that I was having company, I would have prepared more food."

We agree on a place and time to meet in the morning, then shake hands again. The one believer and two skeptics go back to their vehicles.

I forego my meditation and yoga this morning and do some dumpster diving at daylight. I had gotten permission from all three building owners to do so. I taught all of them, and we are on a first-name basis. I find what I am looking for on the third try. Both items get bagged and tagged. Two blocks from the center of town, I undertake a stationary surveillance. I am talking like Erin in my head.

Like clockwork, Officer Barney Williams appears and hastens towards the main intersection. Certainly not as exciting as the morning before, but all the same, he must be proud of himself. I watch until he leaves my view to direct traffic during the morning rush hour. I cross the street and walk in to see Vickie Scudder scrolling on her cell phone. I figure she catches up on her social media while Barney curses people not paying attention to his hand signals and whistle.

"Hi, Yvette. Where's Barney?" I give her a chance to pretend she was not wasting the taxpayer's money by calling her from the doorway.

She shoves the phone under the desk. "He went to direct traffic. He'll be back in about forty minutes."

"I wanted to talk to him about the big arrest. I certainly didn't see that coming."

"I can't remember when we had a double homicide in town."

"Come to think of it, neither can I. How well did you know Brian and Jake?"

She shrugs. "They were older than me. I never hung around with them."

"What about your older sister?"

Again, the shrug. "Maybe. We are six years apart. I never hung around with her, either. She didn't want to be seen with me when we were growing up. I embarrassed her."

I muse with her to get a reaction. "I taught Brian and Jake. It's so sad."

She nods. I think she'd rather be checking out TikTok right now. If she had spent time reclining in Jake's truck, I am not getting any inkling of it. When Vickie was younger, what you saw is what you got. I never knew her to hide her feelings.

"Well, I know you have work to do, and I won't bother you anymore. Could you have Barney call me? I had a quick question for him."

"No problem, Mrs. Strong. There's one other thing."

I turn and face her. "What's that?"

"I heard them talking." She pointed her thumb over her shoulder. "They won't admit it, but you were right to want to look at Dawson's death."

The distance in language using Jake's last name instead of calling him Jake cements my thought that Vickie and he were not watching the submarine races down by the river. "I knew Jake pretty well from around town and didn't think he could shoot himself. Thanks, Vickie." I smile and leave her to her videos.

Walking to Mike and Yvette's house, I know I have the opportunity to ask a few questions now that the police have arrested Jason Stillman for two murders. I will remind them that a rank amateur pushed the cops to re-investigate Jake's shooting and to look harder at the supposed accident that crushed the life out of their other classmate, Brian.

Mike would have a fit if he knew that I was meeting with Simon Stillman and his brother's legal defense team in about an hour.

I knock on their front door. Mike answers. "Hi, Mrs. Strong. Can I help you?" He's wearing baggy gym shorts and a T-shirt a size too small for his ripped physique.

"I just wanted to clear the air with you and Yvette. It was a little frosty at Brian's graveside service."

"Us too, I guess. Now that they made an arrest and all... come on in. I'll get Yvette."

He points to the sofa, and I sit. The TV is on, and I watch as a heavily made-up woman with lots of plastic surgery hawks a super-duper vacuum cleaner. For half-price and three easy payments, it can be mine.

"Hi, Mrs. Strong," Yvette says as she points to Mike to use the clicker to mute the shrill huckster on the shopping channel.

"Dare I ask?" I ask.

"Doc says that she will induce me Monday if I don't deliver by then. The baby is fine on all the ultrasounds, and all my vitals are good."

"Sounds like somebody wants to make a grand entrance."

Pleasantries asides, one of us has to speak next. I can wait, but I choose to move it along.

"Guys, I hope that we can be friends again. I know that by helping Sharon and Mabel out, it might have had us looking at things differently. Mike, you were only looking out for my best interests, and I do very much appreciate it."

Yvette speaks for both of them. "But if you didn't push the cops to take another look, then both murders would go unpunished, and the killer would have gotten away with it."

Wanting to keep the make nice-nice words flowing, I say, "You also helped me look at things differently as well. I asked Wesley and Erin what it was like growing up in Milford with me being a teacher in town. Remember, we talked about Becky Steele and how Milford was like a fishbowl for her?"

"I remember," she says.

"I talked to my kids, and they gave me their different takes. I never thought there was an issue. I was wrong. You could say the same for Vickie Scudder, the Mayor's daughter. She has to be careful in town too, I imagine." Neither Yvette nor Mike gives me any sign they know anything about Vickie.

"Exactly," she says.

"Just one thing bugs me, and it's what Becky said to me at the Dawson house that day."

I have them both hooked now, and I just have to reel them in if I can.

"What's that, Mrs. Strong?" Mike asks.

"Becky said that Jake killed himself rather than get married to Sharon. I mean, of all the reasons for Jake to kill himself, Becky offered that reason. Does that make sense to you?"

Neither Yvette nor Mike makes eye contact with me. I have struck a nerve. I push a little harder. "I rode with her to Brian's service, and we talked a bit." I think they want me to tell them what they already know. "I didn't ask her what she meant. I think it's still a difficult subject." The silence is deafening. I finish with, "But I definitely got the sense that growing up a pastor's daughter in a small town affected her." I can hear their collective sigh of relief.

"But Jake didn't kill himself. Jason Stillman killed him," Mike responds but doesn't answer the question.

I wait a few beats as if I am taking the obvious answer in. "So, are we good, guys?"

"We are, Mrs. Strong." Yvette answers.

"Take care, dear." Looking at Mike, I add, "Here is my number, put me on the call list."

He does as I make my way to the door. My phone rings from a number I don't recognize.

"Hello?"

"Mrs. Strong, this is Barney. Vickie just gave me your message."

I wave the phone at Mike and Yvette as I scurry outside. "Thanks, Barney. I have a quick question that will not compromise your investigation into Jason Stillman." I plow on without giving him a chance to object. "Both Brian Yelito and Becky

Steele told me she was too drunk to drive that night, and that is why he drove her home from the party."

"Okay," he says. He is not committing to an answer, just acknowledging me. I get it.

"But he told me she forgot her purse at the cabin, and he had to drive her back to fetch it. When they went back inside is when they discovered Jake dead."

"That's what he told me, too," Barney says.

"You had them wait outside for the State Police to arrive."

"Yep."

"How long until the State Police released them to go home?"

"They let them go around two in the morning. Why?"

"Was she sober enough to drive herself home?"

"By then, she had calmed down, and she didn't appear drunk."

Barney wouldn't let a drunk drive home if he could prevent. He might have even offered to give her a ride. I don't want to think too deeply on that. "Thanks, Barney. I never asked Brian when I had the chance and I didn't want to remind Becky of that night, so I thought I'd ask you."

"Sure thing, Mrs. Strong."

"Another thing, Barney."

"What's that?"

"If I find anything else out, I will let you know."

"I think we can handle it from here," he chuckles.

"I'm sure you can, Barney. I'm sure you can. Thanks again."

I have my answers, and I am ready to move forward.

CHAPTER TWENTY-SIX

The defense attorney has an interesting way of starting conversations. Erin gave me the skinny on her. Stillman picked the best from the city. She was a former federal prosecutor before hanging out her own shingle as a criminal defense attorney handing big cases.

"Mrs. Strong, that FBI agent you worked with last year in New Haven said I should listen to you. She has quite the track record."

I am blushing as my cheeks tingle like the time I spent too much time on a sunny day pulling weeds in my garden. "You are no slouch either, Attorney Rosenthal."

"Call me Diane."

I return the courtesy. "Gwen."

"Well, Gwen, we have everything set for tonight. Mr. Spencer belongs to two excellent international private investigator associations and started the ball rolling last night to get the experts and the equipment here today."

Diane Rosenthal is a visual person, I note from the metaphors she uses. I say, "It is better that we act out the timeline tonight and you'll see where I am coming from. Not only will you be able to create reasonable doubt, but I will have a viable alternate suspect for you."

Poor Ken had to sit through a dinner with his two favorite women yakking about their own true crime investigation last night. Erin gave me talking points on how to engage with a criminal defense attorney.

Both the attorney and her investigator sit up when I say, "As I point things out to you, Mr. Spencer can preserve the evidence and properly notate the chain of custody."

"Are you sure you have not done this before, Gwen?" Diane asks me.

"Positive. You only got this case yesterday. I've been working on it for over a week." I recount for her where I've been and who I've talked to, then give her a summation of my observations and conversations.

Both of them keep their heads down as they write furiously, Diane on a legal pad and Spencer in a detective's notebook. The only sound is my voice and the flipping of pages. I talk for over an hour and end with, "There are advantages to working and living in a small town. I taught kindergarten to most of the kids involved and watched them grow up." I hold off on telling who I think killed Jake and Brian. I want the evidence tonight to speak for itself.

Diane looks at her investigator and says, "When was the last time you heard such an excellent, non-biased recollection of the facts of an investigation?"

"Would you like to come work for me, Mrs. Strong?" Bill Spencer says. Silver-haired with an average build and a face you wouldn't take notice of in a crowd, he has his own reputation as a teacher of investigative interviewing. His website carries links to headlines about murder acquittals and wrongful conviction exonerations. A heavy hitter and Rosenthal's primary investigator, he's a believer now too.

They take their time clarifying points with me. Bill concentrates on who else to talk to and what to ask them, while Diane wonders how all this would be presented in court. Both stare at the timelines on the wall in my office. Ken had lugged up a couple of dining room chairs for them to sit on and TV trays to set their briefcases on. Everyone has hot coffee to drink. Both snap pictures of the timelines with their phones.

"Now it's our turn to tell you what we know," Diane says.

Bill begins with, "Jason purchased the handgun at a gun show in Alabama last year. He says he gave it to Jake as a gift for the work they were doing on the Mustangs in the spring. He gave Brian one, too. Both were legally purchased. He has a concealed carry permit, but only transported them in the boxes they came in. His fingerprints and DNA are on the bullets, ammo clip, and the grip of the gun."

"We do not contest Jason owning the guns," Diane says.

"I think Sharon McGrath will vouch for seeing one in Jake's bedroom dresser long before his death. I don't know where Brian might have kept his," I reply.

"Next is the Mustang." Bill opens his notebook, flips back some pages, and says, "Since there was one there still being worked on at the shop, it was easy for the police to trace it back to its previous owner by the VIN number. He said that Jason contacted him to see if he would sell it as is. Jason offered him quite a sum of money, and they made a deal."

"I am not sure if the body shop kept records of the Stillman vehicles, since they paid in cash," I opine.

"We don't think so," Diane tells me.

"Jason had a car carrier come pick up the wreck, and the driver paid the owner in cash. They took possession of the title with the seller's signature and delivered the wreck to J&B's Auto Body," Bill says.

Diane closes the loop on the red pony. "Technically, Jason is not supposed to sell the vehicle to a buyer on an open title. He is supposed to be the buyer and then becomes the next seller. He was allegedly avoiding paying sales tax on the resale. It's a misdemeanor in this state."

Diane and Bill look at each other, and Bill says, "They weren't dealing in stolen cars. That was just plain BS."

"But on the other hand, what he paid for the cars and what he then paid to fix them up didn't always get covered by what he sold them for," I prod.

"Right. He made enough on some to cover some of the losses on the others," Diane tells me.

I am sure there is more to where those cars went, but it doesn't sound like the police will locate them. "Were the police able to find the records on all the buys and sales when they raided the compound?" I ask.

"Jason kept no records, I am told," Diane says.

"So, the police only know about the one car, but they know that Jake and Brian fixed quite a few Mustangs for the Stillmans from word around town, and what Candace probably told them."

"That's about right, Mrs. Strong," Bill says.

"And they have no alibi for the night that Jake died except they were watching a Rambo movie at home at the time in question," I say.

"That's true," Diane says.

"Are they saying that Jason's truck at the auto body shop just before Brian died puts Jason at the crime scene?"

Both nod.

"But what about the black older model Honda Accord?"

"They can't identify the driver. We are told it was not at the scene for very long and that possibly the driver didn't go looking for Brian and assumed that he went out for a coffee break."

"Twelve minutes is an awfully long time to hang around an empty body shop. That's weak."

"We agree," she says.

"Did Simon give you footage from the ATM across the street?"

Diane wiggles a disc at me.

I look at my timeline. "Jason's truck was there for less time than the Accord."

"You are correct."

"But Jason has the time to kill Brian after Brian is seen moving cars on the lot, and Brian is not spotted by the driver of the Accord who spends more time on the site? That makes little sense. Unless…" I pause.

"Unless what?" Diane asks.

"They want him for something else," I say.

"The murders give them probable cause to search and to look into their other dealings," Bill says.

"That's why if we can knock out the State's case at the probable cause hearing, they would be hard-pressed to keep investigating my client."

"And vis-à-vis, his twin brother."

"Exactly," Diane replied.

To be safe, I call and get permission from Mabel to visit the cabin tonight. Wouldn't want to have old Mr. Chalmers calling the cops on me. My head is buzzing with the possibilities. If everything lines up as I hypothesize, I will chat with the person I think killed Jake and Brian the following morning. The lawyer and the private investigator leave me to my thoughts. They have to finish putting the props together for tonight's show and tell.

My phone rings. I recognize the number.

"Hi, Dad. What's up?"

"Are you sitting down, Gwen?"

My heart rate shoots to the moon. "Is everything okay?" I try to think what could be wrong with my father or stepmother. They are in great health.

"Yes, we are fine. I didn't want to alarm you, but I received a Facebook message from a woman claiming to be your half-sister. Actually, she said she was Eleanor's daughter and asked me if I was acquainted with Eleanor when she was a nurse in England in the Sixties and Seventies. I said I was, and she asked if she could FaceTime with me. I had one of the people here talk me through that. It is amazing how that technology works. We can do that with the great grandkids, you know. Anyway, she and I talked for about an hour. I gave her your name, and she probably made a Facebook friend request with you already."

"What did she have to say?"

"She didn't know about us until yesterday, when her mother told her."

"I see." My mind is reeling. I have more family that I didn't know about. I honestly never got past my mother 'abandoning' me to think about what her life was like after she bailed on my father and me. Since my self-reckoning, I still needed to constantly forgive her for what she had done. I hadn't gotten any further in that process. My meditation and yoga time got taken up by the Milford murders.

"There are some things better heard from her than repeated by me. Just keep in mind, she was just as surprised to learn about us as we were about her," he tells me.

I hang up, then check Facebook, and sure enough, I see the friend request. We don't look the same. She is younger, shorter, darker, and heavier than me, but I see she smiles in almost all her photos. Try as I might, I can't find any photos of my mother on her feed. My heart rate is still thumping in my temples, and I respond affirmatively. She replies quickly and asks to FaceTime too, then my phone alerts me to the incoming call.

"Gwendolyn, that is a pretty name," she starts. Her accent is noticeable, and it'll take time to get used to.

"Hello Brenda, how are you?"

CHAPTER TWENTY-SEVEN

It's a tight squeeze. Old Mr. Chalmers, myself, and the audio technician are standing in Mr. Chalmers' bathroom. The window is closed as it was on the night of the murder. I am standing in his bathtub and Chalmers is by the toilet. At fifteen minutes before midnight, we stare at each other. Nothing.

The technician says, "Just a blip. You would have to be a dog to hear that." Five minutes later, at the time Chalmers would have been relieving himself during the commercial break, we all hear a pop, like a firecracker going off.

"That's what I heard the night the boy committed suicide," Mr. Chalmers says.

"Thank you, Mr. Chalmers. A fellow will come by in a few minutes and take your statement." I step carefully out of the bathtub while the technician finishes breaking down his equipment.

As we leave the cabin and walk across the moonlit grass toward Jake's cabin, a car pulls next to Jake's truck. Just as I figured it would.

I stand outside the cabin with the driver. She is one of Spencer's operatives. She says, "It's all on video with a time stamp. I left here at eleven-forty on the nose, pulled onto her street, then turned around to drive back here. I did exactly the speed limit. I will start my statement and give Mr. Spencer a copy of the video." If Brian took Becky home, they would have arrived seven minutes earlier than the 911 call.

Six minutes after midnight, a second car pulls in. Bill's other operative gets out. "Eleven fifty-two, I departed Brian Yelito's driveway and drove straight here as quick as I could. It's all on tape." He writes out his statement.

The timing lines up just as I suspected.

At twelve twenty, Wendy Gallo arrives.

"Thank you, Wendy. I know this is going to be strange, but let's walk in."

I follow her in. Bill's female operative goes to the bedroom from behind us. We see an anatomically correct dummy seated at the dining room table. Its head is resting on the table.

"Oh my God, it looks all the same," she says.

I touch my nose.

"Yeah, it smells the same. It smells like gunpowder."

"Where was Brian standing?" I ask.

She points, and Bill Spencer moves into that position. The cameraman and audio-technician swivel their equipment towards him.

"What did he say to you?" I ask.

Wendy replies, "'I didn't want to touch him. I think he's dead.'"

Bill repeats, "'I didn't want to touch him. I think he's dead.'"

"And Becky?" I ask Wendy.

"She was bawling her eyes out in the bedroom."

On cue, the female operative mimics the sound.

"Louder," Wendy says. The operative complies.

Diane and the film crew stand in the living room as the operative wails in the bedroom. I note where Bill's crime scene tech has already dusted for fingerprints and swabbed for DNA on the window, at both the top and the bottom. I see a race car pillow with two holes and goose feathers sprinkled on the floor between where the gun lay on the ground and the window.

It all fits, I think. Two shots. Awfully hard to shoot yourself twice.

∽

I am seated in front of a desk at the Bantry Insurance Agency in town. The person who should be sitting on the other side has not arrived for work yet. It's not quite nine. The darkening clouds outside tell me that the forecasted rain will come sooner than later. I am excited but relaxed. I know the whole story now and I am eager to tell it. I won't be asking any questions or looking for any other answers. I am carrying a recording device to make sure there is no defense argument about entrapment.

There is a fancy sound alert/pepper spray combo in my purse in case something goes sideways. Erin gave it to me this morning. What a thoughtful daughter. She and the kids are doing their schooling at Grammy Strong's house today. Darren and Wesley will join us later in the day. This is going to be a big day for a couple of reasons.

I examine the fire marks along the wall behind her desk. In olden days, a policyholder would place a fire mark on the front of their house. In case of a fire, the insurance company's fire brigade would see the mark and try to put the fire out. If you didn't have one, tough beans. Ken is a collector of these marks. When you work on old houses, you never know what you are going to find in the basement.

I was adamant to Diane that I was not acting on behalf of either the police or her. I had this visit planned since the day the goose feathers stuck to my skirt. I would have had this conversation eventually, but I hope that things will play out the way I think they will.

Becky walks in carrying a satchel and cup of coffee. "Hi, Mrs. Strong. Mrs. Bantry said you wanted to talk to me." She sets the jumbo coffee down after a sip and sets her satchel on her credenza. I notice her blue eyes quizzically appraising me. She is wearing a matching blue dress and sensible shoes. A tiny gold cross hangs from her neck. "Did you find a car and want to get it insured?"

"Not exactly, Becky. I am here to fill you in on what happened to Jake and Brian."

"The police arrested Jason Stillman. That's old news."

"First you told me that Jake killed himself rather than get married to Sharon the following morning."

"Well, I guess I was wrong." She reaches for her coffee and turns on her computer monitor.

Waiting for eye contact, I proceed. "I always thought that Jake was shot before the wedding on purpose. The shooter didn't want Jake to get married."

"Why would Stillman want to do that?"

"He wouldn't, and he didn't."

"What are you saying, Mrs. Strong?"

"I am saying that I know who killed Jake, and I have a pretty good idea of who killed Brian."

"Really, who?" Becky tries to remain cool and goes through her log-in procedure. I wait until I have her eye contact again. She is one cool customer. I can't see her legs under the table though, but I bet her feet are tapping away.

"You made it obvious to everyone when you came on to Brian at the rehearsal dinner and then later at the cabin. The excessive drinking was just an act. You were just acting drunk. After all, Becky Steele would never make a play for Brian Yelito. He was a nice kid, but not the brightest bulb in the chandelier." I tweak her by addressing her in the third person.

"What are you trying to say, Mrs. Strong?"

"What I am saying is that you were trying to make Jake Dawson jealous."

"Why would I do that?" she scoffs, but she knows what I'm about to tell her.

"Jake never told Sharon who he was cheating with, but he swore that the cheating stopped and that it would not happen after they were married."

"I still don't see what that has to do with me," she says.

"Jake and Brian were best friends since kindergarten. They had few secrets between them." I see that I struck a nerve as she props her elbows and tents her hands in front of her face. "Besides, you didn't fool Barney Williams down by the river that night." I am stretching here, but I score another point. "He didn't want to get the Reverend Steele's daughter in trouble." This girl killed two of my students. Maybe I can play it rough too.

"I don't know what you are talking about."

"You don't, Becky? After Brian left Jake's cabin, you returned and pled with Jake to keep your secret relationship with him going. You had expected him to tire of Sharon and he would break the engagement, but he didn't. When you threatened to stand on the altar the next day and out him as a cheater, he told you that Sharon and he would ask you to leave the ceremony. That infuriated you. Oh Becky, I remember how you were in kindergarten when you didn't get your way. I know what your temper is like. When I talked to your father about this, he tried to turn it around that somehow things were my fault. So, when you lost your temper, you went to his dresser and took out Jake's gun."

"Nothing like that happened."

"He was seated at the table when you came up to him in a

rage and pressed the gun against his head and shot him. Only problem, it was on his left side, and Jake was right-handed."

She sits back in her chair, shaking her head. "You've got it wrong, Mrs. Strong. I loved him. I would never kill him."

Finally, an admission. "But you watch cable TV, and you know there was no gunshot residue on his left hand. But it *was* all over your hand."

"No."

"You took his hand and wrapped it around the grip. You couldn't fire another bullet into his head, so you opened the window to shoot that bullet out the window, but you didn't want it to make a big noise, so you went to the bedroom and grabbed his pillow.

She is pressing her hands over her ears. "That isn't true. You're lying."

"You wrapped the pillow around his hand, and you pointed the gun and pillow towards the window, and you squeezed the trigger again. Bang!" I startle her.

"You're crazy. I can't believe you are accusing me of killing Jake." The anger in her eyes reminds me of that day at the Dawson house after the burial.

"You took the pillow out to your car. Then you closed the window and called Brian."

She stands behind the desk. "Get out. Get out now." She is barely keeping it together.

"You convinced Brian to return to the cabin and to tell the cops the BS story that he drove you home, and that you had forgotten your purse and had to go back. That's when you both supposedly discovered Jake dead. You told him to lie for you, that your father would never accept you being at Jake's cabin alone. After all, you had to keep up your reputation as a good girl. It must be tough swimming in a fishbowl, Becky." I play that card now just as I had hoped to.

She shrieks, "Leave now or I will…"

"What? Call the police?" I point to the phone. "Go ahead." I get up and stand by the door. "One last thing, Becky. When Brian called you that day and said that he was going to tell me the truth about not taking you home that night, you couldn't let him do it. That's when you raced over to the auto body shop and tried to persuade him to not to tell me, and that got him killed."

She opens the door to the office with all the composure she can muster. "You can't prove a thing," she says coldly.

"You're right, Becky. I don't have access to your phone records or that pillow. I still have more work to do. And I have a feeling the next person you will talk to will wear a badge and a gun." I enjoy that last parting shot as I sail past her. She needs to feel vulnerable.

I weave my way through the busy office, phones ringing and people talking. They all probably think I was pairing my car and homeowner's insurance for the discount. No one pays attention to me as I slip out the front door. The rain is coming down hard. Ten steps later, I am in the back of Spencer's surveillance van, and he spirits us away.

From around the next corner, we take a wait and see position.

Diane is seated next to me. "Let's hope this works," she says, while Bill is watching two monitors closely.

"I am not sure she was listening at the end," I say. "She was pretty upset." It's only now that my nervousness ramps up. I force my tightening chest muscles to relax. I take in deep, slow breaths. I only see stars behind my eyes for a second before returning to an alert yet calm state.

Two pole cameras are recording the back parking lot of the insurance agency. The images on the monitors in the van's rear are in hi-def color. We don't have to wait long. Becky hustles out the back door of the agency, dodging puddles. We watch her look around for yours truly. Satisfied that I am not lurking in the shadows, she walks directly to the dumpster, lifts the lid, and leans her chest against the angled steel opening. I know from experience that it's going to leave an ugly stain.

She pulls plastic bags and cardboard boxes from the interior and throws them on the ground. Then she backs away from the dumpster, clutching her prize.

Barney Williams appears in the upper left corner of the screen, while Detective Shafer appears in the opposite corner. A third uniformed officer moves in from a hiding spot behind the dumpster. Bill zooms in. Becky is clutching to her chest the practice NASCAR pillow we used the night before, along with a dirty orange rag borrowed from the body shop.

Like scared prey, Becky pivots as the officers close the distance around her. She tries to feint and get them to commit. Barney moves like a lumbering bear, and she tries to run past him. The former high school defensive end dives at her and tackles her around the waist. They roll around a bit, but he outweighs her almost three to one.

Becky's hair is soaked, and her blue dress becomes saturated. All the cops drag her to her feet, then they handcuff her.

Barney leads her to his cruiser. It's his collar. I am glad I called him from the cabin the night before to schedule the meeting between Rosenthal and Shafer in the wee hours of the morning. All nay-sayers are now yay-sayers. It's a good feeling.

"Bingo!" Diane exclaims. "Thank you, Rebecca Steele."

CHAPTER TWENTY-EIGHT

"I am going to move to the other room now. Brace yourself," Brenda tells me.

I've hooked up my laptop to the big screen TV in our living room. I watch as the camera lens faces down towards my half-sister's shoes and finally jiggles to a fixed position. As the picture comes into focus, I stare at the emaciated figure propped up in a hospital bed. The last time I laid eyes on my birth mother was over a half-century ago. The unsmiling face of a young woman from those black and white photographs is unrecognizable now after several bouts of fighting, and now losing to, cancer. She is frail, just skin and bones hidden under a flowery housedress. Brenda filled me in on her condition and said that our mother didn't want to go back to the hospital again, so they converted a room in Brenda's house to be her hospice.

My mother wears a skullcap. I imagine that the chemo burned out all her hair. An air tube is affixed into each nostril. My mind is all over the place. Is this really my birth mother? Or some complicated hoax to scam us for money? Those fleeting doubts disappear when a reedy, thin voice fills the living room. I clutch Ken's hand as I hear it. There is no doubt she is Eleanor.

"Gwendolyn, you look beautiful, and who is this handsome man?"

"This is Ken, my husband. We've been married for thirty-three years."

"What do you do, dear?" she asks Ken.

"I fix up houses for people in town," he replies.

"Brenda told me you were a schoolteacher, Gwendolyn."

"That's right," I say. "Did you continue with nursing when you returned to Jamaica?"

"Yes, and then I volunteered at the children's clinic for a time, until I got sick."

You would think that after a fifty-year separation that we would have more to say, but I was warned that her energy is failing, and we would have to keep things brief.

"Gwendolyn, the doctors tell me that my time is short. I asked Brenda to find you so that I could tell you how sorry I am for leaving you and your father when I did." I can see that saying this is so hard for her. Brenda comes back into the frame and holds our mother's hand.

The words I longed to hear ring in my ears as I stutter, "I forgive you, Eleanor. For years, I thought that I did something to make you angry, and that is why you left us."

"No, dear, you were a wonderful child, always so happy and full of energy. It had nothing to do with you."

"I understand that now and know that you had a hard time back then."

She said, "Those were difficult times. My parents were very strict." She pauses. This is difficult for her. "When I told them I was pregnant and was going to marry a white man, they disowned me and stopped talking to me. They told no one about my situation. My mother and father were ashamed of me. I was twenty-one years old and living alone in England. I had nobody except your father."

"I can't imagine what that must have been like," I admit.

"It all became too hard on me, and that is when I saw that you and Stanley would be better off without me. I was not in a good way."

I have nothing but compassion for this old woman, breathing her last breaths and using what energy she has left to make amends with me. "It must have been very hard for you," I say. And with that, the last vestiges of my anger and resentment fade away.

"A day didn't go by that I didn't think about you, Gwendolyn. I always wondered how you were doing. As time went on, I was too ashamed to try to reach out to you. I am sorry. I should have done this sooner."

She and I are crying. Ken is fighting back tears. Finally, I put a coherent thought together and say, "I am glad that you told Brenda about me and that we have a chance to visit. Would you like to meet your grandchildren?"

I call Wesley and Erin into the room. On the screen, Brenda sits next to my mother, and her three kids go to the other side of the bed. Then Erin calls in Darren and my grandchildren. Brenda's grandchildren fill out the rest of our TV screen. Eleanor and I sit back and let everyone talk and get to know each other.

Eventually, Brenda sees that our mother's energy is waning. This chat is exhausting her.

Brenda gives me the high sign. Her clan moves off screen, and only my mother is left in the center of the screen. Mine do the same and I say, "There is one last person here that wants to say hello."

I wave a kiss to her, and she waves one back to me. It lands on my wet cheek. "Goodbye, Mom."

"Goodbye, my precious daughter," she replies.

Ken and I move off screen and stand nearby as my father sits down where I had been warming the couch. Ken is holding me tightly, lest I might topple over.

"Hello, Eleanor," he says. I can hear in his voice that he wasn't prepared for how she looks. "It's been a long time."

"Hello, Stanley."

Our family has a quiet lunch after the video chat. Wesley and Erin understand, but I am not sure the little ones know that we were saying both hello and goodbye at the same time.

Ken and my dad get busy on a leaky bathroom faucet. Saint Darren takes my grandchildren back home. Erin and I have so much to catch up on. The rainstorm has moved on, the dark clouds give way to clearing skies. Emotionally, I am like a wrung-out dish towel. Our feet walk us to our favorite spot. This is a place we've come to for twenty-five years. We just enjoy the quiet for now.

Milford Elementary has been shuttered since the school closing. I can't believe that decision was made just a few weeks ago. At some point, they will have to winterize the building. At least they are still mowing the grass. The flower beds around the flagpole needs weeding. I will leave a message for Mary Meade after hours. I'm sure she will appreciate it. We silently trod behind the school to the rear parking lot and off to the far side to the swing sets

The town's insurance company argued that the monkey bars, slide, merry-go-round, and swings were too dangerous to stay. The words "attractive nuisance" were bandied about, but the townspeople, many of whom had hung upside down from these monkey bars, told the school board where they could go when it was suggested that the cherished welded-steel creations be removed.

In the end, a compromise was reached, and the playground was covered with wood chips.

We sit on the swings and gently sway back and forth. We face each other as we talk.

"I would have liked to be a fly on the wall when Attorney Rosenthal told Shafer and Barney they had the wrong suspect," Erin says.

"Actually, she let the video of the re-created crime do most of the heavy lifting," I say.

"Smart."

"The police knew that they would see it again at the probable cause hearing if they didn't accept the findings as presented."

"Shafer could be a hard ass, but I think he'd rather get it right than get totally embarrassed," she added.

"Then she provided them with an exhibit-quality timeline. One of her paralegals pulled an all-nighter doing that."

Erin was impressed. "Stillman's attorney wants to stop them from snooping into the twins' affairs. I think that was her goal from the outset."

I smile. "Then like turning one card at a time from a good hand, she gave them old Mr. Chalmers statement, the acoustic findings of the sound of firecracker, which was actually the muffled gunshot, and the statements of the two drivers who tested the story Brian had given Barney about taking Becky home, and finally the pillow I had retrieved from the dumpster."

"What about the rag?" she asks.

"Becky must have used it to hold the handle when she released the hydraulic jack. Her DNA would be all over it. Otherwise, why would she have taken it?"

"That rag from the body shop and her car on ATM video is hard to explain away," Erin says.

"The motive is harder to establish for killing Brian than it is for Jake, but when they show the video of her at the body shop, she might give it up."

She says, "What jury wouldn't draw that inference?"

"The cops gave Diane Rosenthal a hard time about me going in and talking to Becky, but when she explained how I was going to confront Becky at the insurance agency, they saw the logic. If Becky went out to the dumpster to retrieve the evidence, they knew that their case against Stillman would deflate like a two-day-old birthday balloon."

I reach into my bag and show her a framed 8x10 glossy of Becky clutching the pillow I had stitched together from the bedspread swathe. "I am going to put this up on my wall in the office. The private investigator, Bill Spencer, dropped it off for me as a present while we were talking with my birth mother."

"I'll do the same for you with a copy of tomorrow's headlines," she says.

"We should go see Mabel and Sharon and tell them what happened. They should hear it from us and not some nosy reporter fishing for a quote," I say as I dismount the swing.

"What about your buddy, Simon Stillman?" she says as she leaps off the swing and lands lightly on her feet

I turn to Erin. "I want you to stay away from him. I purposely didn't tell you what I think they were doing. If anything ever happens to me, there is a letter addressed to you in our safe deposit box. You need to give it to your friends in the FBI. Simon knows about it, and we have a handshake agreement that I won't say anything and he'll leave us alone."

"What if the cops want to keep investigating them?"

"I can't do anything about that, but I will not help them more than I already did by tipping them off about the Mustangs."

We walk towards Sharon's apartment. I know we are going to rock her world. Mabel, I am afraid, will just say thank you, but she knows that her son is gone forever, and nothing we say or do is going to bring him back.

My thoughts drift back to meeting my mother after so many years.

As if she's reading my mind, Erin says, "It took a lot of courage for your mom to tell her family about you. She kept that secret from her daughter for decades."

"I could see how much she regretted not reaching out sooner."

"Had you ever thought of contacting her?"

"Yes, but those thoughts never started out good and always ended badly. I had so much anger and a sense of abandonment, I could never bring myself to do it. Instead, I just channeled all that negative energy into doing positive things for you and Wesley."

"And your students," she says.

"I realize now that I gravitated to kindergarten because I was my students' age when she walked out on me and your grandfather. I never wanted you kids and my students to feel they were alone or abandoned."

"Do you think you would have worked so hard for Jake and Brian if it wasn't for your mother leaving you the way she did?"

"Tough question, honey. I have to meditate on that," I say seriously. "There is so much for me to think about. It's not every day you solve two murders and get reacquainted with your mother whom you've been estranged from for fifty years."

"I know exactly what we should do after we talk to Sharon and Mabel," she says.

I smile. "A large pepperoni pizza?"

"Let's invite Dad and Grandpa too," she says.

I love this girl.

CHAPTER TWENTY-NINE

I have the whole row of seats to myself. Just then, the airliner breaks through the clouds and the entire cabin is bathed in sunlight. A blanket of white as far as the eye can see below, and bright blue skies above. I can't imagine how pilots don't get excited every time they do this. Like Greek gods, they streak towards the heavens.

We don't fly often (mostly to Disney World when the kids were younger), and I still get a thrill on take-offs and punching through the clouds. Landings, not so much.

Ken and I talk about going places, but then we fall into our usual routines, and we forget about it. Milford is where we live and work. Our entire family is within a few neighboring zip codes. We have four seasons and welcome each one—well, maybe not the freezing winters. But then again, how can you truly celebrate the explosion of colors in the spring without going through the long, dark winter nights?

I wasn't surprised when Brenda called me yesterday and told me Eleanor had died overnight. The hospice care and a clear conscience made her transition peaceful, my half-sister explained.

The family asked me to come to the funeral, and I said yes. I am flying to Miami with a change to Kingston.

Two plates of Emelina's chocolate chip cookies are carefully stowed in a plastic container in my luggage. She said that she is serious about selling her cookies from the yoga studio, and she asked me if I knew anybody that would want to learn all of her secret recipes.

The day before I received the news of my birth mother's passing, the whole town was abuzz with talk about Becky Steele's arrest.

Both Barney Williams and Detective Shafer shared the press conference podium. They explained how new evidence surfaced, implicating Becky in both homicides.

Diane Rosenthal made the right noises about how the police never stopped investigating to find the truth and their diligence proved her client innocent of the charges. Jason Stillman agreed to plead guilty to a misdemeanor. As a first-time offender for not signing the title to the Mustang still sitting at the body shop, he would most likely get probation, community service time, and a fine.

Once the correct gas tank was fitted on it, Jason agreed to give it to me. Zoom zoom! It will be ready when I return. Ken is jealous. I told him he can drive it occasionally. A candy apple red Mustang V-8 convertible is a guy's ride, but this girl can have some fun too, right?

My man is working on getting the materials for Abe's restoration and kitchen build-out. This will be a nice job for him as the weather turns colder.

On a more somber and telling note, the Reverend Jeremiah Steele couldn't get into his church's sanctuary fast enough when the TV reporter ambushed him that morning. He flung a terse "No comment" over his shoulder before slamming the red door shut.

While waiting at the airport today, I received a text message from Mike Strohmeyer. Yvette gave birth to a healthy baby girl overnight. *"Nine pounds, twenty-two inches, ten finger and ten toes, looks like her mother, thank goodness. One more thing. We named her Gwendolyn, and we would like you to be her godmother."*

This is not the first time someone's favorite kindergarten teacher has been asked to do that.

Gotta love small towns.

The End

Want more Gwen? Follow the clues with Milford Coal & Ice, book two in the series Milford Coal & Ice

Two bodies are found hidden behind a fake wall. Emelina's Nephew and his wife disappeared 50 years ago. Can Gwen heat up this cold case?

ALSO BY J A HODA

Milford Connection Gwen's origin short story

What is supposed to be a fun weekend at the pizza capital of the world, New Haven, Connecticut, turns out to be the beginning of small town kindergarten teacher Gwendolyn Strong's amateur sleuthing origin story. A twenty-year old murder is being investigated by a podcaster using a closed Facebook Group of amateur sleuths when things turn deadly. An undercover FBI agent approaches Gwen and her daughter to assist in the growing investigation. Someone desperately wants past secrets to stay buried and will stop at nothing to stop the agent's team of cast-offs and amateurs. As the investigation deepens, we see Gwen's gifts come to fruition right up to the exciting climax **FREE DOWNLOAD**

https://BookHip.com/GPZGAMA

What's next for Gwen? Two dead bodies are found behind a fake wall in the basement of a pre-civil war era mansion. The grisly discover rocks the world of centenarian Emelina Bidwell who believes her nephew and his wife left small town Milford fifty years ago. Former kindergarten teacher Gwendolyn Strong agrees to help her mentor, but the sleuthing rules are changed by Emelina who made promises of secrecy to the dead all those decades ago. Can Gwen solve the mysteries of their deaths with one arm tied behind her back? Who is protecting the killer a half-century later? Why does the town's power elite want to shut her down? Is she next to disappear? Can this amateur detective repeat her success In this second book of the small town mystery series

Buy ***Milford Coal & Ice*** (Book two) and follow the clues as Gwen heats up this cold case.

Milford Coal & Ice

Sift out the clues with Gwen. A nut allergy almost turns deadly at Milford's daffodil festival. When former kindergarten teacher Gwendolyn Strong starts delving into the elderly woman's claim that someone is trying to kill her, little does she realize that the killer won't stop until they get what they are after. Is it revenge? Is it money? Things get deadly serious when they make an attempt on Gwen's life. Does Gwen have the courage to continue sleuthing? Will she be able to be able to figure out who it is before they strike again?

Buy *Milford Daffy Day* (Book three) and follow along with Gwen as she finds more ingredients of this killer's deadly recipe.

Milford Daffy Day

Milford Bed & Breakfast is scheduled for release December 19, 2022
See the cover at https;//jahoda.mailerpage.com

ABOUT THE AUTHOR

J A Hoda graduated in 1975 with a B.S. in Criminology from Indiana University of Pennsylvania.

Hoda is a former Police Officer, Insurance Fraud Investigator and for the last 25 years has run a successful Private Investigations business. Many of his cases have made the headlines of the Philadelphia Inquirer and the New Haven Register.

He sat on the boards of the both the National Association of Legal Investigators and the CT Assoc. of Licensed Private Investigators. John is a Certified Legal Investigator and a Certified Fraud Examiner, retired.

He was feted as a debut novelist, panelist, and judge for the Shamus awards at the Mystery Writers of America Dallas Conference in 2019 with his first in the six-book FBI Agent Marsha O'Shea Series.

Hoda produces and hosts a weekly podcast: My Favorite Detective Stories at www.johnhoda.com where he interviews crime fiction writers about their flawed fictional detectives.

He has won publisher awards for articles in The Legal Investigator and has written numerous articles for PI Magazine and other publications. He created the DVD: The Ultimate Guide to Taking Statements. He is a frequent guest blogger and webinar presenter on Investigative Interviewing. He has written four how-to books about the business side of private investigations and coaches PIs how to survive and thrive at www.ThePICoach.com

John answered the writing muse in 2013 with his debut novel:

Second Chance at Bat. An average Joe though luck and circumstance gets a one in a million chance to play in the Major Leagues.

Through the years, Hoda told stories about his latest cases over coffee, at parties or at dinner engagements. Asked repeatedly to write them down, he finally did with: Mugshots: My Favorite Detective Stories

He was feted as a debut novelist, panelist, and judge for the Shamus awards at the Mystery Writers of America Dallas Conference in 2019 with his first in the six-book FBI Agent Marsha O'Shea Series.

John has been a lifetime athlete, playing club soccer and semi-professional football, running marathons, and bicycling long distance.

His other creative activities include stand-up storytelling and writing, producing, and acting in amateur theater.

He can be reached through his website https://jahoda.mailerpage.com or hodagen@gmail.com

facebook.com/JAHodaWriter
twitter.com/johnahoda54

ACKNOWLEDGMENTS

Dave Pasquantonio for holding my hand during all edits and revisions.

Ruth Koizim for the extra set of eyes on the proofreading.

100 Covers for getting the covers perfect.

Susan Krauss, Pamela Tournier, Ilona Schmidt and the Fairfield Scribes for the deep dive critiques and encouragement.

Printed in the USA
CPSIA information can be obtained
at www.ICGtesting.com
LVHW040737220124
76933ILV00044B/629